J
ELL

Elliott, Laura.

Flying south.

$15.99

FLYING SOUTH

Laura Malone Elliott

FLYING SOUTH

HARPERCOLLINS*PUBLISHERS*

Although the references to historical events and national figures
are factual, Alice and the characters and situations in *Flying South* are
fictional. Any resemblances to true life are coincidental.

Flying South
Copyright © 2003 by Laura Malone Elliott

www.harperteen.com

Library of Congress Cataloging-in-Publication Data
Elliott, Laura.
 Flying South / Laura Malone Elliott. — 1st ed.
  p.   cm.
 Summary: In Charlottesville, Virginia, amidst the social and political
turmoil of 1968, eleven-year-old Alice learns when to fight battles and
when to let go from her family's elderly gardener, Doc, and begins to
connect with her widowed mother.
 ISBN 0-06-001214-5 — ISBN 0-06-001215-3 (lib. bdg.)
 [1. Mothers and daughters—Fiction. 2. Gardening—Fiction. 3. Race
relations—Fiction. 4. Single-parent families—Fiction. 5. Charlottesville
(Va.)—History—20th century—Fiction.] I. Title.
PZ7.E453 Fl 2003
[Fic]—dc21

                                      2002014414

Typography by Amy Ryan
1 2 3 4 5 6 7 8 9 10

First Edition

*To the memory of my parents,
Edith and Jack,
and their magnificent rose gardens*

"Hope" is the thing with feathers—
That perches in the soul . . .
   —*Emily Dickinson*

CONTENTS

Prologue

There are different kinds of good-byes. A lot of them. There's the see-ya kind, when you'll bump into that person tomorrow and pick up right where you left off, midchat. There's the good-bye-good-riddance kind, when you meet some snotty kid at summer camp and you're *really* glad that you'll never see her again. And there's that sick-to-your-stomach-but-wasn't-it-wonderful kind of good-bye. The good-bye that changes your life.

I learned about that last kind of good-bye from Doc. Doc was a very old man, our family gardener, and my best friend. I wouldn't tell Bridget that—she still thinks she's my best friend even though we haven't seen one another for almost a year now. She claims only babies spend time with adults. "Never trust anyone over 30," she says, copying the college students. But I don't think that's right. Doc might have gotten mad at me, but he'd never have dumped me just because another girl told him to. And he knew a lot of stuff: old stories, ways to make plants and people grow, ways to see that a thing's season is done, ways to survive hurts that crumple up your heart. Last summer, the summer of 1968, he pretty much taught me most of the important things I know about life.

I try to share some of what Doc taught me with the kids at school. After all, we're going into junior high school this fall. We're old enough to understand the world. But they don't listen. They're too busy playing Beatles records or trying on white lipstick. And there's been so much going on this past year. Who can keep anything straight? As if killing President Kennedy back in 1963 hadn't been bad enough, last summer another crazy man shot down his younger brother Bobby while he was running for president. Plus, some redneck killed that nice preacher man Martin Luther King, Jr. His assassination made the nation crazy. There were riots in cities all over the country. White folks around here were scared half to death, even though nothing happened around Charlottesville.

Boys are dying in Vietnam—boys not all that much older than I am. When I ask why, grown-ups talk about "commies" and "dominos" and sip their cocktails with a worried look. The Communist threat is something everyone takes real serious, especially from the Soviets. We've all got a stash of canned food in our basements in case Soviet Russia drops the bomb and we have to hide from the fallout—or if the student riots spread out from college campuses—or if the Black Panthers really do bring about revolt.

It's been a pretty scary year. About the only good thing coming up is that they're actually planning to land a man on the moon sometime soon.

I'm sorry Doc won't be around to see that space launch. He would have thought that was "the cat's meow." That was his term for when something was groovy. I think a lot about the things he used to say, especially last summer.

CHAPTER ONE

*never forget
whose grandchild you are*

I was nasty hot early on last summer, the summer of 1968. As early as June, houses hummed and rattled with the constant *whrrrr* of window fans. The air stayed thick and humid well past sundown. It was suffocating, like spending the entire day in a steamy bathroom. Such weather makes people ornery. Doc and I got into a lot of arguments.

Our first squabble came right after school closed. The sun was already too mean for children to roll around in the yard, so I was hanging on the screen door of the back porch, watching the mockingbird dive-bomb our cat and waiting for Doc to come up from the garden for lunch. The screen had a soft, easy bow from years of my leaning against it. I was pushing my nose into it, to print a grid into my skin, and tasting the screen's rust with my tongue when Doc walked up through the boxwood.

"Alice, what do you think you're doing?" he snapped.

I hadn't stopped when I saw him coming. I would have stopped immediately had I seen Mama. But Doc was one of those remarkable grown-ups who respected a child's experimentation. Usually, he would have asked me what the screen tasted like. I would have answered that it tasted like cold metal with a bite.

Instead, I muttered, "Nothin'." I stepped back from the screen and opened it for him. It *thwacked* closed behind us.

"Don't you realize you could get tetanus from doing that? What if you cut your tongue on the wire?" He eased himself onto the whitewashed wooden bench by the kitchen table and pulled off his sweat-soaked straw hat.

"What's tenatus?" I asked.

"Te*ta*nus. A terrible infection that can lock your jaws together and give you convulsions and make your nose fall off."

"Really?"

"Yes, really."

I fell silent and tried to rub the screen imprint from my nose. Doc knew about these things. During World War I, when he was a teenager, he had run off to fight

6

in France. When the army discovered he was only sixteen years old, it put him to work in field hospitals away from the trenches and the battles. He learned a lot about infections and medicine. That's where his nickname, Doc, came from.

I was about to ask if he'd ever had tetanus when Edna announced that lunch was ready. Edna was the lady who took care of Mama and me. She fixed our meals and kept my dresses ironed just the way I could stand them, with only a hint of starch. During the summer, she cooked lunch for Doc and me. Today, she put down bowls of chicken salad, kale, and beets. Doc had grown the vegetables in our garden. She whispered to him as she leaned over the table, "You really shouldn't tease her, Mr. McKenzie. She's just a baby, you know."

Edna sat down on the bench beside me. She smelled sweet, of vanilla and talcum powder. We all bowed our heads in silent prayer. I wished they'd say grace out loud because I never knew what to say when it was left up to me. This time, though, I asked God to keep my jaws from locking together.

When Doc lifted his head, he glared at me. He didn't like getting into trouble with Edna.

Doc and Edna went way back. They had worked for my grandmother for decades. Edna had run the house while my grandmother ran the garden club and the local chapter of Daughters of the American Revolution and the volunteer library league. Doc kept the gardens fruitful during the Depression. My mother had kind of inherited the responsibility for Doc and Edna, just like she had inherited our family farm deep in Virginia's "president country," the green lands rolling just east of Charlottesville, around the homes of presidents Jefferson, Monroe, and Madison.

Mama had a weird relationship with Doc and Edna. Sometimes she listened to them carefully and gratefully, like they were parents. Other times she bossed Edna and Doc around, politely enough, I guess. Either way, she didn't seem comfortable with her role, like she had on a hand-me-down coat that itched her all over.

Take the week before, when Bobby Kennedy had died. He was leaving a party celebrating his winning the California primary when someone walked up and shot him in the head. It was beginning to feel like anyone who talked about peace or getting along with others was going to get killed. Like Martin Luther King, Jr. They'd gunned him down in April. It was really frightening. I know I wanted all the company I could get during Bobby Kennedy's funeral. But Mama had sat, all quiet and stiff like, in the living room, watching the television news cover the service. Edna stayed in the kitchen, tuned to the radio, crying while she dried the dishes. I couldn't understand why they didn't listen to the reports together; they both seemed so sad.

Doc interrupted my ruminating.

"She should know better, Edna," Doc said as he

plopped a hunk of butter onto his steaming-hot kale. It made a pretty, little pool of gold in the leafy emerald greens.

He turned to me. "What would your grandmother have said if she had seen you looking like poor white trash, swinging on the door with your tongue hanging out? Don't ever forget whose grandchild you are. Miss Margaret was a great lady."

"Yes, sir." My goodness, he was crotchety. I didn't like it. When I was real little, my daddy had crashed and died while test-piloting a jet plane for the air force. The only thing I remember about him is a big grin and the smell of pipe tobacco. Mama spent most of her time on the tennis court now. It was important that Doc and Edna like me. Very important. I tried an old trick.

"Doc, why do birds fly south for the winter?"

Doc glanced at Edna and smiled. I had asked him this riddle at least a dozen times since I had heard it. I suppose he knew it was my way of trying to smooth him out.

"I don't know, Alice." His voice had gentled and his eyes smiled. "Why?"

"Because it's too far to walk."

"Hah-hah-hah-hah." Doc's old dentures *slurp-slapped* against his gums as he laughed.

CHAPTER TWO

*things have
a time of beauty*

Doc? Hey, Doc?"

Two weeks later, I couldn't find Doc anywhere. Not under the cherry trees. Not in the apple orchard. Not by the shed. Not under the pines.

I was getting worried. It was early morning, the cool time of day, when sunshine was still velvet soft and lacy shadows from the maple trees skated back and forth across the lawn. Doc liked to be busy then, weeding, hoeing, and picking. In the afternoon, when it was crazy hot, he mostly sat and drank glasses of Edna's lemonade.

I circled the hill to the back of the house, and there I spotted Doc by the rose beds. He was sitting in his wooden wheelbarrow in a heap of spent blossoms he had cut—a hulking old troll of a man soaking in a rainbow pool of soft petals.

As I approached, I heard him talking to himself. I stopped to listen.

"Never felt that before. Not now, Lord. The vegetables are coming in good. Miss Grace has that party of hers. I've got to get the roses in shape for that. She don't know diddly-squat about roses."

Doc held a huge red blossom. He stuck his long, mottled nose into it and sucked the scent in hard, like old ladies did with smelling-salt bottles.

"You okay, Doc?"

He dropped the rose and grunted. "Of course. Why wouldn't I be? Why are you forever sneaking up on people, child? Polite people announce themselves."

"I'm sorry." I fished around in the rose petals and let some cascade like a waterfall—pink, red, lilac, white, tangerine, yellow—over his thick knee. "Can I help prune the roses?"

Doc *never* let me touch our 124 rosebushes. He said if I cut them wrong, I'd stunt the bloom. He'd only let me pick Japanese beetles off the leaves. I had to drop them into a coffee can filled with gasoline. The gasoline killed them. I hated the job. The beetles' prickly feet stuck to my fingers. The gas stunk. But I did it, so I could stay with him. Edna was usually busy in the kitchen, and I didn't like baking. I never knew for sure where Mama was. The nearest girl to play with was three farms over, down Route 22. And I never really hit it off with girls my age and their endless games of Barbie. I mean, how many times can you change a doll's outfit? Doc was company.

This day, I got lucky. He looked at me funny and handed me the shears.

"Really? You'll really let me?"

"I'm going to teach you to do it proper, Alice. It's time you learn some ladylike hobbies."

"Can I cut a whole basket of flowers, too, Doc? Can I?"

"I suppose so, if you listen to what I tell you."

We walked to the rose beds that ran in colorful swags across our yard. Doc shuffled to a stop at a pink rose tinged with yellow called Little Darling. Despite its prissy name, it's one of the hardiest roses there is. It could easily survive my clumsy pruning. Doc was no fool.

"First, cut off the overblown blossoms. Right, Alice?"

"Right." I reached for one, then stopped. "Why is that, Doc?"

I like to know the how-comes for doing a thing. That often annoys adults. "Because I say so," is their usual answer. But Doc appreciated being asked.

"Because their time of beauty is over," he explained. "All they do now is burden the bush. Cut off the spent blooms, and the bush will keep sprouting new blossoms. One of the hardest lessons to learn, Alice, is how to recognize when a thing's time is done."

I nodded, tucking away the info without really understanding it.

We cut buckets of blossoms that were starting to brown and rot and tossed them into the wheelbarrow. "Deadheading," Doc called it. Doc paused a moment to wipe his face with his white handkerchief even though I couldn't spot sweat on him. Any trickle of perspiration disappeared into the furrows of wrinkles on his tough, old, crocodile face.

"The more you challenge something, the more it produces," Doc continued. "The more you cut a rose, the more it blooms. Some roses will give you flowers from May through October if you spend time on them and know what you're doing. If you ignore them, they won't amount to nothing. Sort of like children." I grinned when he said it. I'd come to recognize such moments as his way of teasing me.

We surveyed the bush. This Little Darling stretched its thorny arms higher than my head and as wide as our fancy new double-door Frigidaire. There must have been fifty blossoms on it clustered in groups of three or more. The air around it smelled spicy and happy.

I spotted about twenty blooms that would look beautiful on the front hall table. Every three or four days, Doc filled a cut-glass vase with fresh buds so that their scent was the first thing we smelled as we came down for breakfast. I knew we were due for some fresh roses. Wouldn't it be wonderful to tell Mama that I had picked them myself? She kept her lipstick stashed behind the vase so that she could freshen her makeup on her way out the door. She always paused for a moment to smell the roses, her pale, china-fine face framed by their colors. Those were the best moments to catch her for some conversation.

I played the scene out in my mind:

"Good morning, Mama," I'd say.

"Good morning, Alice. What are you up to today, sweet pea?"

"Nothing much," I'd answer.

"Don't be bothering Edna now. She's making a special dinner. A new beau is coming. If I decide I don't like him, I'll pass him down to you."

"No'm," I'd answer. "I'll play outside."

That's about how all our morning conversations went. But tomorrow *my* roses would be there, waiting to catch her attention. She would lean over and inhale some of their sweet scent. Smelling a new-cut rose, grown up in the sun, is like breathing in early-morning life. It'd soften her right up.

She'd say, "My, just look at these blossoms, Alice."

"I cut them for you, Mama," I'd say proudly.

"You did? Why thank you, honey." She'd catch me up for a long, *real* hug, not one of those quick, for-show ones. "They're beautiful, just like you, Alice."

Yep. I could hear it, taste the compliment, sweet as a peppermint. It'd be lovely.

Doc pointed to a blossom that was just opening. "Here's a good one. Cut it where it's long enough to go into a vase and hold itself up and just above where you see a branch of five leaves. That way a new shoot will sprout right there."

I cut it and held it as carefully as if it were spun glass.

"Go ahead. Put it in water." Doc nodded encouragement. After six blossoms, he stopped hovering so much. He grunted his approval and added, "When I go, don't you let these roses die off, Alice. I've taken care of them for near thirty years. They're . . . well . . . they're important. All I've got to leave you. You understand, child?"

"Sure, Doc. Don't worry. But you're not going anyplace anytime soon, are you, Doc?"

He just patted me roughly on the shoulder, then pointed to another blossom cluster. "There's a beauty, Alice."

We cut a couple dozen, making a pink mountain in the basket. I tried to pick it up, but it was heavy. Water sloshed all over us.

Doc always hated it when I spilled milk at the table. I didn't want anything to spoil the nice time we were having. I apologized quickly. "I'm sorry, Doc. Did I get your shoes wet?"

He grabbed my shoulder and squeezed hard. His eyes squinted mad.

"It's only some water, Doc," I stammered.

He scared me. He was hurting my shoulder. Doc couldn't really be that mad over some water, could he? All the same, I squeezed my eyes shut and braced myself for a nervous slap, like Mama gave me now and then when I made the mistake of pestering her while she dressed for an evening out. It never really hurt. I just hated seeing her hand coming down on me.

I could hear Doc breathing hard. I held my own.

But nothing happened.

I peeped open an eye.

Doc wasn't even looking at me. He was staring over my head toward the vegetable garden. There, squatting on his haunches like a frontier scout contemplating a trail of tracks, was a groundhog.

CHAPTER THREE

sometimes the sun makes a person mean

This was not just any groundhog, of course. This was Doc's GD groundhog, the one that was eating up all his tomatoes before they even turned pink.

He was huge, almost as big as our springer spaniel, Mac. When he steamed through the wildflower field, he squashed all the black-eyed Susans flat.

He and Doc had been sparring for years. The groundhog had fathered many a generation of babies that Doc had run off. But Doc hadn't been able to rid himself of this granddaddy groundhog. He was just too feisty. I'd seen Doc sic Mac on him, and Mac was usually game for taking on anything—fox, raccoon, stray dog twice his size. But the one time he took on the GD groundhog, Mac turned tail and ran. He wouldn't come out from underneath the porch until Edna laid out a soup bone.

Personally, I rooted for the groundhog. I know it was disloyal of me. But the groundhog had been around so long I thought he kind of belonged with us. Edna and I had nicknamed him Big Tom. We'd never tell Doc that, though. The four things he hated most in the world were possums, Japanese beetles, Richard Nixon, and this particular groundhog.

As we watched, Big Tom sashayed up to the nearest cornstalk, ripped off an ear, and peeled back its casing. Then he sat back, chewing on the kernels, as happy as a preacher at a church barbecue.

It was more than Doc could bear.

"Alice, you hide behind this wheelbarrow and don't move, not an inch."

I crouched without argument. I wasn't too worried for Big Tom. I had seen this duel before. The groundhog would outrun Doc easy.

Doc grabbed a hoe from the wheelbarrow and crept around the edge of the garden. It always amazed me how fluid his movement was when stalking the groundhog. Usually, he creaked and lurched like a wind-up robot that had seen better days.

There was no wind blowing to carry his smell and tip off Big Tom, so Doc made it to about ten feet from him. He stood up straight and hollered, "HEY!

HEY YOU!" Doc swung the hoe around over his head. "Get out of my corn!"

The groundhog took one more leisurely chomp out of the corncob before dropping it. Then he just sort of trotted off—*trotted*—showing Doc he wasn't the least bit afraid of him. He was a bodacious critter, that ground-hog. I couldn't help but laugh.

Maybe it was the insult of that trot that hardened Doc to really getting him this time.

Doc started running, a bumpy, out-of-practice jog that jangled all his loose change out of his overall's pockets. "Hey, you fat rat! I'm going to get you."

The groundhog stopped, turned, and chattered his big front teeth threateningly. Those teeth could bite through Doc's hand in one chomp.

Doc brought the hoe down—*THUNK!*—missing Big Tom by inches. That started the showdown for real.

Now, the groundhog ran. Doc lumbered behind. They headed into the wildflower field and down the other side of the hill, so all I could see was the hoe swinging and glinting in the hot sun.

This was serious. I'd never seen Doc keep after him this long.

I stood up. "Run, groundhog, run. Run for your life!" I started after them.

The wildflowers were in a swirl from their chase. I could hear Doc panting and Big Tom grunting and the *thunk* of the hoe as it missed, hit the soft earth, and stuck. With each *thunk*, Doc cursed loudly.

"Run, groundhog, run!" I screamed again.

Out of the daisies darted the groundhog. He shot past me, his shiny fur surging in waves with his muscles and rolls of fat. He headed for the open yard, right for the croquet course I had set up. He took a bad turn, and for a minute, a hoop stuck to his head before it flew off.

Doc came thundering behind, like a rhinoceros pumping along the Savannah.

"Go back to the house, Alice!" His breath was coming in raspy blasts. But he kept on running. He was moving faster than some of the forty-year-old guys my mother played on the tennis court.

They were heading for the highway that sliced along our back acres. Big Tom must have lost his bearing in his fright. If he had any sense, he'd have headed for his burrow. No matter how mad he was, Doc couldn't squeeze down the hole after him.

"I've got you now!" Doc shouted.

My stomach twisted when I realized Doc was trying to chase him into the road where he'd be hit by a car racing toward town. I couldn't believe Doc would be that cruel. It would be a horrible way for Big Tom to die, smashed and broken.

"Run, groundhog, run!" I was crying as I ran. I don't know what I was crying for, the groundhog or for Doc's lost sense of right and wrong.

Somehow I managed to pass them both and get to the fence line first.

"Stop!" I screamed. I flapped my arms. "Stop, you stupid groundhog! Go the other way! THE OTHER WAY!"

Big Tom scrambled to a halt between us.

"Alice, get away from here," Doc snarled. His face was purple. His straw hat was gone. His hair was standing up like a thistle thatch.

I shook my head. "No."

"What's the matter with you? Move!"

"No."

"Move, or I'll kill him right here in front of you." He shook his hoe at me. I'd seen him kill a huge black snake with one blow of that hoe.

I swallowed hard. "No."

"This GD groundhog eats my corn! MOVE!"

A truck screamed by, racing from Richmond to Charlottesville, rattling the earth. We turned to look, startled by the blast of its horn at me, standing, stupidly, right by the road. When we turned back, the groundhog was gone. Just vanished.

Doc flattened. He swayed where he stood and balanced himself on the hoe. Within seconds, he had turned from a garden gladiator to a winded, doddering old man.

"Doc, I'm sorry." I ran up to him. "Are you okay?"

He stared me down silently. Then he shuffled toward the house.

"Doc," I ran after him. "Let me get you some water."

He ignored me. I had betrayed him. I felt horrible.

All I could do was run to the house for Edna to fetch him some lemonade.

He wouldn't speak to me for the rest of the day. I'm not sure I would have come up with much to say to him anyway.

I'd known since I could recite the ABCs that Doc could be crusty, but I always figured it for bluster. Like an old dog that has to bark at everything to prove he can still hear and scare off danger. It'd never occurred to me that Doc could have a mean streak running through him. I didn't want to believe it. Instead, I passed it off to the heat. The sun had baked his brain for the day. It can do that, you know.

CHAPTER FOUR

you gotta talk to a person to get an answer

At least I had the roses Doc and I had cut for Mama. But my conversation with her didn't go so well either.

It started off right enough:

"Morning, Mama."

"Morning, Alice."

But it didn't go anywhere after that. Mama turned her head back to the mirror and continued tracing a berry-red line across her lips. Her face and hair were so fair the red yanked your eyes right to Mama's mouth. I guess that was the idea, but I never did like the look of lipstick unless someone was in full smile. Bright red on a scowl was scary.

I hung on the banister and swung back and forth, waiting.

Mama pressed her lips together and popped them open to seal the coloring. "Stop swinging. You could pull the balusters out."

"What are balusters?"

She sighed and leaned over to do her mascara. "Those white poles that hold up the railing. I certainly don't need to be having them repaired. Last time I had the carpenter here, he gave me a hundred and one reasons why he couldn't fix the cabinets the way I wanted. No one ever talked to Lyle that way."

Lyle was my father.

"Why not?" I asked.

Mama turned to look at me with a smirk. "Because, baby doll, your daddy was a man."

"What difference does that make?"

"All the difference. With banks and workmen anyway. Lord, Alice, I guess we have to have a talk."

She plopped herself down on the steps, her pleated tennis dress doing a little flip. She straightened me up and put her hands on my shoulders. I prepared myself to learn some great mystery of life.

"You know, Alice, I've only got a little money left from your grandmother, and the money that comes from the air force can't keep this house up. I don't know a thing about . . ." Mama suddenly frowned. "What in the world have you done to your hair?"

24

"My hair?" What was wrong with my hair?

She pulled a comb out of her pocket—the woman was forever pulling bobby pins and combs out of thin air—and roughly yanked at the crown of my head.

"Where in the world do you get this cowlick?"

Mama's hair was golden and silky and sleek. Mine was mud-brown with waves that liked to glob up in tangles. She tried to pull her comb through it. I waited for my whole scalp to yank right off; she was combing so hard. I tried not to yelp.

As she tugged, she looked me over. She didn't like what she saw. "When was the last time you washed your face? . . . You've got dirt behind your ears. . . ." She stuck her comb back in a pocket and looked at my hands. "Let me see those fingernails. . . ."

With a heaving sigh of disappointment, she dropped my hands and said, "Go take a bath."

"But Mama . . ."

"But Mama nothing. You're a sight. You better not look like this tonight. Mr. Barker is coming to dinner."

I'd heard about Mr. Barker. She'd been out with him a lot lately. But I'd never actually met him. This meant Mama was pretty interested in him. It was her way of showing off how she—(Edna, really)—ran our house. I hated these dinner rituals because I needed to be spit-and-polish, too.

She was still talking. "He's very respectable, Alice. A lawyer. On the town council. A lot of political promise, they say. His father—or maybe it was his grandfather—anyway, one of them was a member of the University of Virginia's secret seven. Old Virginia family, you know." She had a weird pucker about her face when she said the final words, like she wasn't sure she liked the taste of them.

Quietly, she added, "We need to put our best foot forward. You know that, don't you, sugar lump? Can't have people thinking we're not presentable. Men like presentable wives and children. It's hard enough keeping men interested when they figure out how old you are and how old that makes me."

"But Mama . . ."

She pushed me toward the stairs. "March."

Mama checked her watch, rolled her eyes, and patted her perfect Faye Dunaway hair. "Now! Make me a pretty girl to come home to."

Out the front door she scooted, banging the screen door on her tennis racket.

She never even noticed the roses.

I took the bath. I still had the cowlick.

Edna was in the kitchen, her gray head bowed as she worked biscuit dough. It was yucky, sticky work on a hot summer day. In the winter, she'd put the bowl of golden dough on the radiator to rise, and the whole house smelled of sweet melted butter and yeast. Now the kitchen just stunk of sweat and flour. I knew she was suffering through making it because company was coming.

She stopped kneading the dough to fan herself. "What's up, honey bunch?"

"I can't do anything right. Everybody's mad at me. Mama thinks I'm dirty, and Doc thinks I'm a traitor and . . . and . . ." I tried to think of something Edna hated me for but couldn't.

She smiled at me. Edna understood everything or at least acted like she did. She had four grown children, another two she'd lost to polio, and thirteen little grandchildren who all seemed to end up at her house on Sundays. Edna was sweet forgiveness. She just didn't have the time to spoon a whole lot of it on me. I understood that. She got to our house by 7 o'clock—early enough to fix breakfast, make the beds, clean the house, do a wash, and hang out the laundry to dry before lunch. She made that meal and the fixings for dinner before going home at 3:30, our house left spotless and inviting. She didn't move fast, but she worked steady and constant the whole day through.

"Why don't you go find Mr. McKenzie? Bet he could use some help."

"He isn't talking to me."

"Aw now, Alice, you've gotta talk to a person to get them to answer. You tried sweetening him up some? You catch flies better with honey than vinegar, you know."

"Right," I muttered.

"G'on now. Go try."

I found Doc by the old chicken coop. We just used it for storage these days. Its white paint was peeling, and an enormous patch of violets grew around it in the springtime—I suppose the result of all that free chicken fertilizer years ago. I couldn't figure out why he was down there until I saw the hose in his hand.

One of the GD groundhog's dens was underneath that coop. Doc had been trying to flush him out.

As I got closer, I realized that Doc had put chicken wire over the entrance to the burrow. He wasn't trying to flush out Big Tom. He was trying to drown him.

I bit back a cry of dismay and decided to be cool. "Whatcha doing, Doc?"

With a grunt, Doc turned and headed back up to the house to shut off the water. I circled the coop. Doc had covered one back entrance and the next one, too. They both were full of muddy, coffee-brown water. I felt clammy until I checked the stump, fifteen feet behind the coop. Maybe Doc hadn't noticed that tunnel. I'd only found it one day by accident, when I'd been pretending to be that Venus statue—the one with her arms missing. I fell off the stump, smack into the hole.

The hole was open. I looked across the pasture and saw Big Tom waddling away, his shiny fur matted down by water. Relieved, I darted up the hill to find Doc.

He was rolling the hose into a circle on the toolshed floor. I wasn't going to mention the groundhog unless he did. I was trying to forget about his warpath on Big Tom.

"Whatcha going to do now, Doc?" I asked.

No answer.

"Can I help you?"

He shot me one of those sideways I'm-not-speaking-to-you glances and stomped past me.

I followed as he pushed the wheelbarrow toward the rosebushes in front of the house.

"Mighty nice morning," I prattled. "The radio said it was only going to be in the high-eighties today, Doc. Isn't that nice? Might even get a breeze to breathe. That would be nice, wouldn't it, Doc? Don't you think so, Doc? Doc?"

No answer except for the *ku-thump, ku-thump* of the big wheel bumping over mole holes and fallen sticks.

Doc stopped at the first rose bed. He turned his back on me.

Honey wasn't working, so I tried vinegar. I started pulling off leaves and tearing the satiny green to shreds. Each yank sent the bush shaking. Normally, Doc would have scolded me mightily for it. But he still ignored me.

I was about to give up when I heard him groan. He'd leaned down to pick something off the ground under a bushy rose with tangerine-colored blossoms. He had kind of creaked over and caught himself with his hands. Now he was struggling to straighten back up. *How could a human body get so stiff?* I wondered.

"Here, Doc, let me help you." I grabbed his elbow

29

and pulled. He shook me off as he stood upright, but at least he looked me in the face.

"You want to help me, Alice?"

"Yes, sir," I beamed.

"Lean over and pick up those leaves. You see them? The ones that are yellow and dotted?"

"Yes, sir." I reached through the stalks of the thick bush carefully and picked up about a dozen yellowed, curled leaves. They were speckled with black spots.

"Put them in the basket."

"Yes, sir." I dumped them into a basket in the wheelbarrow. "What's wrong with them?"

"Black spot," he said. "This darn rose gets it every summer no matter how much I spray it. Then it spreads to the other roses. Look at Mr. Lincoln." The tall, dark-red rose named for the Civil War president had just a sprinkling of polka dots on its leaves, sort of the way some children get chicken pox a few bumps at a time.

Doc sighed. "I'll have to spray it tomorrow. And all the others."

It was hard work mixing the chemicals and then lugging the sprayer around from bush to bush. He'd have to pump the canister to get the spray going and then hold the spray nozzle over each leaf to protect it. To cover all 124 bushes, he'd spend hours walking around in a cloud of poison. He was getting awfully old for that stuff.

I also worried about that spray. I'd seen a television program about some lady who everyone was calling a hysteric because she talked about pesticides getting into the food chain and endangering eagles by making their eggs too spongy to hatch. She made a lot of sense to me. I knew Mama had her book, *Silent Spring*, hidden in her nightstand, like it was a trashy romance novel or something. But I didn't mention it to Doc because most government people and businessmen quoted in news reports called her ideas "hogwash."

Instead, I took his hand. "Is there anything I can do, Doc?"

He grunted. "Not unless you are suddenly willing to work hard for a living."

Hurt, I dropped his hand.

"Well, all right, don't be pouting on me." He made his apology by patting me roughly on the head. "There is something you can do, Alice."

I brightened.

"No matter of spraying is going to protect these roses unless I get all the black-spot leaves up off the ground away from their roots. You willing to pick them all up for me?"

If it made him happy with me again, I was game. "Sure, Doc."

"All right then. What are you waiting for?"

CHAPTER FIVE

a girl deserves some pretty flowers

Had I known what I would be up against, I might not have volunteered. All the roses had at least a dozen leaves at their base. Most had *a lot* more. And the leaves didn't drop to the outside of the rose bush in a nice even ring. They tended to get stuck halfway down, pinned on the thorny branches. Or they got tucked in the forks of the fat stalks at the very bottom of a bush. The thorns there were as thick and long as the claws of a tiger.

The first time I got scratched, I didn't even whimper. I didn't the second, third, or fourth time either. But by the time I crawled up under the twentieth bush and had ten long scratches down my arms, I did begin to cry a little.

I think those tears blurred my vision because I can't believe the stupid thing I did next.

I was underneath a Queen Elizabeth that must have stretched six feet across. Its trunk was as thick as a fence post and split off into a dozen branches. It was more like a small forest than a rose bush.

I already had two fistfuls of yellow leaves. I knew I should dump them in the basket behind me before trying to pick up more. But there was just one last nasty black-dotted leaf on the other side of the bush. To dump the leaves would mean having to crawl back up under the bush on my hands and knees to get that one last leaf. My knees already felt like a zillion pins had been stuck in them.

No, I told myself, *get the last leaf and then take a break.* I wadded the leaves I'd collected into my left hand. I slid my right hand through a narrow V of prickly branches toward that one, last leaf.

Careful. Just a little more.

I threaded my arm through up to my elbow.

Almost.

I bent my arm down toward the ground. The leaf still lay just beyond my fingertips. No choice. I inched my arm through the V up to my armpit. My face was right up against a thicket of spikes.

I wriggled my fingers, brushing the edge of the leaf. *Come here, you blankety-blank thing.* I twitched it toward me.

Finally! I got it! I picked up the leaf, sighing with

33

relief. That's when I did the really stupid thing. I jerked my arm back to get out of the V of claws.

A whole jaw of thorns closed in on the tender underside of my arm.

"OOOWWW!" I screamed. "Ow, ow, ow!"

I tried to stand up but bumped my head against a ceiling of bush and scraped up my face. The thorns in my arm only nailed themselves in deeper, locking me in the fork. My forehead burned. I felt a trickle of blood ooze into my eyes.

"Doc! Doc! Help me!"

I thrashed around. The thorns tore down my arm and gutted it. I dropped the wad of leaves in my other hand and tried to pull the branch back, so the thorns would come out of my flesh. All I did was tear up my palm and fingers. A row of thorns found my left ear and sliced it open, too.

"OOOWWWW"! I screamed again.

"Hold still!" a dark voice bellowed.

I stopped, stuck and pinned, like a cub in a bear trap. I could see Doc's feet.

"God almighty," I heard him mutter, and then his boots disappeared.

"Doc? Doc? Don't leave me."

When he thumped back, Doc carried long pruning shears. I could see the metal point swinging by his knees. With heavy grunts, he got himself down onto the ground. His beat-up face slid under the bush with me.

"Don't move now, Alice. You hear me good?"

Doc reached up with the sheers and cut off the thick trunk just below my arm. Half the bush crashed over to the ground, freeing me.

Doc grabbed my good arm and pulled me to my feet. "Come on."

Drip-drip-drip. I looked down. Blood was beginning to dot my white tennis shoes, sort of like the black-spot did the roses. My shoes were getting really polka-dotty by the time Doc shoved the back door open and pulled me to the kitchen sink.

"Lord have mercy!" Edna dropped her rolling pin.

"It's not as bad as it looks, Edna," Doc said.

"Not as bad as it looks?" She elbowed him away. "Men folk always make an accident to be nothing if they had something to do with it."

Doc scowled.

"Go get the peroxide out of the medicine cabinet," she ordered him, giving Doc no chance at back talk.

"Peroxide?" I whimpered. Peroxide frothed and scalded my knees when they got scraped. "Don't use peroxide, Edna." I tried to back up and run.

But she had me by my good arm, gentle yet firm. "Now, honey lamb, I've got to wash out these scratches. I can't tell how deep they are."

She began wiping my face with a wet, cool tea towel, the first thing she could reach out and put her hand on without letting go of me. Mama wouldn't like those tea towels stained with blood. And Doc had had to kill one of his rosebushes to get me loose. Oh, I couldn't do anything right. Tears washed down my cheeks and burned like crazy.

Edna kept cooing at me, talking, washing so I didn't even realize she had a cotton ball rinsed in peroxide before she stuck it to my forehead.

"Ow!" I yelled and squirmed. "Ow! Ow! Ow!"

"I know, baby, I know," she crooned but kept on dousing me.

I finally quieted and endured the torture, soothed by her voice.

By the time we were through, I had three bandages on my face, one on my ear, and a long gauze strip wrapped up and down my arm. Nothing needed stitches, although the slashes were pretty deep and jagged as lightning bolts. The scars weren't going to be pretty.

"There, honey bunch. You're all done. Goodness, what a morning. Would you like me to fix you something special for being such a brave girl?" Edna asked.

"Anything?" I whispered.

She put her hands on her wide hips and looked amused. "Pretty much anything."

I saw a bowl of fresh-washed strawberries gleaming in the sun from the kitchen window. Edna's strawberry shortcake was just about the most wonderful thing in the world.

"Could you make some shortcake for dinner? Please, Edna, pretty-please?"

Edna's shortcake would keep Mama talking to me through dessert. Even when she was dieting, she couldn't resist it.

Edna smiled, flattered, and I realized I should say nice things about her food more often.

"I suppose I could manage to make shortcake for a little girl who asks so nice," she said as she patted my face.

She frowned big-time at Doc as she brushed past him to the pantry. I hadn't realized he'd been sitting there all that time.

Once Edna gave him space, he came up and actually took my hand. "You all right, Alice?"

I nodded.

"You gave me a bad scare, child."

"I'm sorry about the rosebush, Doc. Are you mad at me?"

Doc looked out the window a minute, like he was choking on something. He must have been furious with me. Another tear fell. Embarrassed, I pushed it off my face. What a stupid baby I was.

"No, I'm not mad at you, Alice," Doc said in a voice I didn't recognize; it was so low and so small. "You wait here a minute."

It was more like twenty minutes before he came

shuffling back, carrying a whole basketful of roses. I couldn't believe it.

"A pretty girl deserves some pretty flowers for her room once in a while," he mumbled without looking me in the eye.

"*Humpf*," came Edna's voice from the pantry. But it was a *humpf* of approval. I'd heard it before. "I don't have time to be helping her put them in a vase now, Mr. McKenzie, seeing as how I'm making a *special* shortcake. You come take this bowl and help her."

"Me? I just grow roses. Arranging them is women's work."

Edna emerged from the pantry carrying a big vase. She plopped it into Doc's hands. Winking at me, she said, "G'on now. Fix them on the porch. There's real work to be done in here."

Doc stuck out his lower lip, then shrugged, giving up. That, as much as the basket of roses and his sacrificing his Queen Elizabeth to set me free, told me how sorry he felt.

CHAPTER SIX

*you learn by watching,
trying things out*

Even though he had bad-mouthed it as women's work, Doc was a right good flower arranger. He put them in the vase just the way Mama and Edna did— long stems in the middle with shorter ones circling out front—so that the bunch made a nice kind of Christmas tree effect. He even let me tuck some of them in place.

"Cut them at an angle," he said, clipping the stems into little arrows at the bottom. "That way they'll suck up water better."

He handed me one of the tangerine-colored blossoms, the source of the black-spot. "What's this one called, Doc?"

"Tropicana," he answered. "It causes so much trouble

I'd rip the GD thing out of the ground except the blooms are so beautiful. Look at how straight the stem is. The blossoms stay good for a week, even in August. This rose would win your mother a lot of ribbons if she ever bothered to go to the shows."

My grandmother had entered all the flower shows— for daffodils, lilies, and roses. The desk in the living room was crammed full with ribbons. There was a bunch of silver cups Edna always had to polish that she'd won, too. Mama didn't go in for that stuff. She wore minidresses and sang songs like "Blowin' in the Wind" with the radio.

"You don't like Mama much, do you, Doc?" I asked quietly.

"What? What do you mean?" Doc crammed a string of blooms into the vase before he said anything else. Finally, he spoke. "You know, Alice, each of these roses has a story to tell." He pointed to a beautiful rose with yellow petals edged in pink. "This one's called Peace. It's a Hybrid Tea. Came out of France back in the 1930s, right before the Nazis invaded. The day Berlin fell and Hitler shot his sorry self, they named it Peace."

I hated it when grown-ups tried to answer a question by talking about something else. By the time they got to the point, I'd lost track. But Doc didn't do that much, so I figured he was definitely getting at something. I tried to concentrate.

"Each rose needs something a little different to be its

best," he continued. "Peace here needs lots of water and manure and pruning in the fall. It don't take to shade. You come to learn these things about a rose by watching it, trying things out. When something works, you stick with it. When it doesn't, you look for another way. You gotta have patience.

"I don't dislike your mama, Alice," he said more to himself than to me. "I guess I'm just not finished watching her yet. I can't figure her, no how. When she was bitty, she was a lot like you, following me around, forever asking questions. Then she just vanished. Next thing I know, she was all growed and had your father on her arm."

"Did you like my daddy?"

Doc's face turned hard. "No."

"How come?" Even though I didn't much remember my father, Doc's answer stung.

"A real flyboy, that man. Big swagger. Been a fighter pilot in Korea. Practically stopped people on the street to brag on it. Your grandmother, Miss Margaret, she hated him. It broke her heart when your mama dropped out of that girls' college and ran off and eloped. I swear Miss Margaret never was the same after that."

"Mama and Daddy eloped?" I'd never heard that before. It sounded incredibly romantic. My esteem for Mama shot higher.

"Yes. And a fool thing to do, too. She was only nineteen."

41

If all my father did was brag and make Mama fall in love with him, he didn't sound so bad to me. Heck, Doc bragged on his roses. I decided to push for more info. "What's so awful about that, Doc?"

"Here's what's so awful: the man couldn't settle down. Drank too much. Talked too much. Dragged your mama out west to some godforsaken place where idiots flew suicide missions just to figure out how to make planes go a few miles per hour faster. Miss Margaret and your mama hadn't spoken for three years—not a single word—until the day your mama called and begged Miss Margaret for money. When Miss Margaret refused, your mama completely dropped out of sight."

I swallowed all the information. It was a big swig. After a moment, I asked, "How'd we end up back here?"

"Miss Margaret. She was in Charlottesville when a friend told her how sorry she was to hear about your father's crash. Your grandmother had no idea he'd died. Imagine how embarrassing that conversation was for her. But she was a great lady. She went to find your mama at the desert base she'd been living at. She'd already left. So Miss Margaret had to track your mama down, knocking on neighbors' doors, asking if they knew where her own daughter had gotten to.

"Turns out your mama had moved into a little apartment in Washington, D.C. Gotten a secretary job in the State Department, working off her father's coattails."

Doc fell silent again, but I could tell there was more.

Like, how did I fit into all this? "Was I born then, Doc?"

He took a deep breath and let it out like cigar smoke. "When your grandmother came to the apartment door, a three-year-old child opened it. It was you. She didn't even know about you. I never heard the whole story, but I suspect Miss Margaret convinced your mama to come home for your sake. Your mama never would have been able to provide for you proper."

"I don't remember my grandmother at all, Doc, except that she smelled like gardenias."

"Miss Margaret died a few months later. Heart attack. Probably the strain of having your mama back here. Things were real tense."

It was the longest bit of talking Doc had ever done. But he added one last thing: "You know, Alice, sometimes I think I'm hard on you because I get you mixed up with your mama. She disappoints me. But that ain't fair to you, child. An old man gets confused sometimes. Understand? Truth is, I enjoy your company mightily."

I nodded. I'd have forgiven Doc anything right then, even clobbering Big Tom.

That was about all the soul-searching chitchat Doc could stand. Without another word, he cleared off the leaves and stems from the porch table and left.

I sat and tried to make sense of all he'd told me, especially the information that Mama had cared enough about me to come back here.

I nearly jumped out of my skin when I heard her voice. "Ally, honey?"

I turned around.

"Sweet Jesus." Mama stopped and put her hand on her heart. "What happened to you?"

"It's okay, Mama. I was just helping Doc."

"Do what, in God's name?" Mama stayed frozen in the doorway.

"I was helping him fix the black-spot on the roses. You see, if you don't pick up the spotty leaves . . ."

"What? Don't I pay that old man enough money for him to do his own work?" Mama spun on her heels and stormed toward the kitchen.

I ran after her. "No, Mama, don't be mad at him. It was my fault, not Doc's. I just stood up while I was still underneath the bush. I'm sorry. Really."

Mama kept marching, muttering to herself. "I only keep that meddling old curmudgeon around because I promised Mother. I don't need him here."

"Mama, please, don't yell at him. Please."

"Alice, you let me take care of this. I can't have you getting hurt because he's too old to do his own work and can talk you into doing it for him. There are plenty of college boys in Charlottesville who can do the yard work for half the money and a lot less attitude."

Desperate, I grabbed her arm. "Mama, please! He's the only friend I've got."

"Friend?" She stopped and looked down at me, wincing

at the sight of my bandages. "Alice, honey, he's just a careless old man who let you get hurt. You've got friends your own age."

"No, I don't."

"Oh, come now." She thought a minute. "There's that girl you like to ride with."

"Her parents had to sell their horses."

"Well, what about Elizabeth's daughter, oh, what's her name?"

"Laurie."

"Right. Laurie," Mama repeated the name like she was sticking it into memory. "You two always got along."

"Not anymore. She's Meredith's best friend, and Meredith doesn't like me. So Laurie doesn't like me."

"But there's . . . ." Mama's voice trailed off. There was no one else to think of. She plopped down on a dining room chair. "Lord, Alice, have I been such a rotten mother that I haven't even helped you make any friends your own age?" She took my hand and looked into my eyes. She had such light blue eyes. Whenever she really looked at me, they startled me.

This time, though, there was something about her gaze that made me brave. I reached out to brush back her blond bangs, and she smiled. "You're a good mother, Mama. Doc told me how you came back here for my sake."

Mama's smile melted as fast as ice on a hot stove. She pulled away, and her voice was sharp. "What? That old man was gossiping about me?"

"Not exactly gossiping, Mama. You know how it is with me," I put on a dimpled smile. "I can ask a lot of questions."

Mama laughed in spite of herself. "Yes, you can, Alice. You'd make a perfect diplomat"—she paused, then added with a wink—"or con artist."

"What's a diplomat?" I knew right well what a con artist was and didn't like what she was hinting at.

"Oh," she said as she turned those blue eyes toward the floor. "Someone who makes peace between countries by asking lots of questions with a big smile to get information without people realizing they're giving it. Someone concerned about the state of things."

Something about that rang a bell. "Is that what Grandfather did?"

"You do take in everything, don't you, Miss Ears. Yes, he was the ambassador to Belgium right after the war. But only for a few years. He irritated too many people with his bluntness. So, he came back here and taught political science at the University of Virginia. Mother hated being back. She'd loved all those embassy receptions in Europe. She never forgave him for losing that post. I think she secretly wanted to be an ambassador herself."

"Did he like teaching?"

"I think he liked discussing ideas."

"Would I have liked him?" I asked.

"I don't know that you would have, Alice. He could be mighty tough on people. He was legendary at Virginia for flunking boys out. He always answered my questions with quotations from Shakespeare—like a riddle."

"Would he have liked me?"

Mama pulled me onto her lap. "Probably. But, sweetie, if he hadn't liked you, it would have been because he didn't like me much. My parents were both pretty . . . well . . . let's just say they had expectations that I couldn't match. I was never much of a student, which disappointed my father horribly. He didn't have any use for me because of it. And your grandmother and I, we just didn't see anything eye to eye. It got even worse after Father died, and I became her project instead of him. She wanted me to be ladylike and help tend the cemetery and to marry some boring businessman. You know, a doctor-lawyer-Indian chief," she joked, pointing to my shirt buttons and reciting the nursery rhyme. "And that just wasn't me back then. Now I can see her point more. I'd like to find someone who's settled and sensible and would be able to take care of us."

"Can you tell me about my daddy?"

"Lyle?" Mama sighed. "Well, Lyle was about the most beautiful man I've ever seen." I felt myself blush at the tone of her voice. "He always looked jaunty and wind-blown, like he'd just jumped out of the cockpit of a plane. You look a lot like him, Alice. And he could make

47

me laugh. Lord, he was funny. He was quicksilver, fire, and could talk love to take your breath away. When he took my hand . . . I don't know . . . anything seemed possible. He promised to take me to San Francisco, to New York, to Chicago, to all sorts of places where I wouldn't be known as 'Miss Margaret's wayward daughter: Grace, the disappointment.' "

"So, was it wonderful being married to Daddy?"

I felt Mama stiffen. "It had its days, honey."

"Why didn't you talk to Grandmother after you married Daddy?"

"Darn that old man," Mama breathed more than said. She thought a long time before she went on. There was a lot going on in her head. I could see it.

When she finally spoke, it was slowly, as if each word was a tar baby to get stuck and die on, just like Brer Rabbit almost did. "Lyle hated my mother. The very first time they met, she asked him who his parents were, why he hadn't finished college, what he planned to make of himself, and why he wasn't higher up in rank in the air force. Can you imagine? I think that's what prompted him to propose to me just a month later—out of pure spite for her. After I said yes, I would marry him, Lyle told me I had to choose. 'Her or me,' he said. Well, that seemed an easy choice. She'd always made me feel so bad about myself. And I was so in love with him. So we ran off together, and I didn't see her for years, until she found us in D.C. after your daddy died.

48

"But, you know, Alice, I had moved to D.C. before Lyle crashed," Mama's voice was little more than a hoarse whisper now. "He did some things . . . well, when I was pregnant with you, he . . . I know he didn't mean to, he'd been drinking, but he . . . And then when you were just toddling around, I wanted a nicer place to raise you up. The base was in the Mojave Desert, so remote and hot and dusty. I think I was homesick for green and changing seasons." She paused for a long time. "I guess he couldn't be questioned without feeling I was disrespecting him. I wanted him to leave the air force. It seemed so dangerous, all those test flights. And he'd been passed over for colonel. We had this terrible argument, and he . . . he . . . well, I probably deserved it." Her voice trailed off.

I'd never heard her be so jumbled up. "Deserved what, Mama?"

Mama laid her pretty face atop my head, so I couldn't see her expression. But I saw her hands trembling. "He hit me, honey. That time I couldn't open my eye for two days it was so swollen. . . . I'd been laying into him pretty badly. . . . I said I wished I'd never met him, that my mother had been right about him. . . . After that argument, I left with you, even though I still loved him. That's when Lyle started volunteering to test-fly every crazy plane they came up with. I swear I think he wanted to die in the air. Maybe because of me."

She hugged me tight and rocked us. I didn't dare ask

a question that might make her let go. I tried to will the minute to last an hour. But, of course, it didn't.

When Mama spoke again, she had her sparkling party voice on. "Anyhoo—coming back here meant we could have nice garden parties. Let's go up and pick out your dress for dinner tonight. Mr. Barker's coming, you know. Maybe I'll even let you wear one of my necklaces to pull attention away from all those yucky bandages. Would you like that, Miss Alice May?"

She jumped up before I could catch hold of her again.

CHAPTER SEVEN

*people can run
hot and cold*

I was up in the monster rhododendron bush by the sideporch when Mr. Barker arrived. It was my favorite hiding place. It was as big as a good-sized apple tree, and the big glossy leaves could shield most anything from view. The branches were smooth and easy to climb. I didn't want to admit that they were beginning to bow dangerously with my seventy pounds. I also forgot that my dress was bright ugly orange—neon colors were "in," Mama had said when she bought it—so my plan to spy on him unseen was fated to go wrong.

I liked spying on Mama's dates. How else was I going to learn how to act with men? By watching TV shows like *Bewitched* or *Get Smart*? I told myself I was lucky having a mother who still dated, to show me how it was done. Mothers who'd been married a million years—what could they know about the real world? Sure seemed like a lot of fuss and nonsense, though, the nervousness and stupid joke-telling. Mama had been all aflutter when she glued on her fake eyelashes to get ready for Mr. Barker's visit. One had gotten stuck on her eyebrow at first. Even when she got it right, it still looked like a school janitor's sweeper broom as she blinked. I told her she looked better without it. I meant it as a compliment, that she was pretty naturally. That's when she told me to stop bedeviling her.

She sure could run hot and cold. I'd thought we'd gotten close talking about my daddy. But that's the way some people are, I guess, open the door a crack just to slam it shut real hard. She obviously got uncomfortable talking about him. So I'd be mindful of that in the future. I fingered the chunky ceramic bead necklace she had loaned me for the night to remind myself of what she'd said earlier: "See, Ally, just like girlfriends sharing jewelry."

I figured I'd hang in the rhododendron bush until she called me for supper. That'd keep me out of trouble. She'd just come out to call around the house for me when a silver-blue Cadillac the length of Kentucky pulled itself 'round the driveway.

Mama patted her hair, tugged at her pastel blue skirt, and tucked one foot into the arch of the other to wait for Mr. Barker—just the way I'd seen Miss America do when she posed for photographs.

As the car door opened, the setting sun ricocheted hot and white off it, so I couldn't see anything but glare. I inched forward along the branches, sticking my nose through the leaves. I could make out a tall figure towering over my mother and a loud, deep voice saying, "Miss Grace, aren't you the picture of Virginia beauty."

Well, nice compliment, I thought. But then he did that thing I hate—he grabbed her around the waist and pulled her right up to his side to walk her into the house. She looked like a child all caught up underneath his smelly old armpit. He was saying something else.

I leaned forward to hear.

CRAAACK.

I looked back just in time to see the branch splitting where I clung to it and to hear, "Grace, what's that in the bush over there?"

The branch snapped and I *bump, bump, bumped* down to the ground, taking three other branches and an avalanche of leaves with me.

THUNK. I landed hard, and the ground knocked the wind and one of Doc's curses out of me.

I lifted my chin and watched two pairs of shoes—one big and black, the other neat and light blue—run toward me. But embarassment kept me down. I tried to become one with the ground. I sure felt like dirt.

"Alice, are you hurt?" Mama asked, kneeling over me.

"No ma'am. I'm all right," I mumbled to her toes.

"Then why don't you get up, dear," the icy singsong of her voice told me to move, quick.

I stood myself up, brushing off leaves, bark, and moss.

"Say hello to Mr. Barker. Bill, this is my . . . this is Alice."

I held out my hand, and Mr. Barker crushed it in his huge one before realizing how grimy mine was. He pulled out a bleached-white monogrammed handkerchief to wipe his off. He slapped me with one of those adult, I-am-not-amused-but-I-shouldn't-be-mean-to-a-dumb-kid smiles. "Charmed, little lady, I'm sure."

He took my mother's waist again and turned her to the house. "Does she always hide in bushes?" he asked into Mama's hair. "Is that why she's wearing all those bandages?"

It was the beginning of an entire evening in which I would be mostly talked about rather than talked to.

During dinner, I scooted my plate and glass as far away from Mr. Barker as I could to keep myself out of trouble. By dessert time, I was almost at the other end of the table. I was concentrating happily on my strawberry shortcake when I became subject matter again.

Up until then, I'd pretty much blocked out most of their conversation. It'd been typical boring, grown-up fuss about all those fool college kids: Who do they think they are, criticizing the president? Don't they realize they're lucky to be in college to begin with and to be born Americans? Ship them all off to fight the Vietcong, and then maybe they'll change their tune about how rotten the glorious United States of America is, by golly. You know, that type of ranting.

I kept glancing at Mama, watching her like Doc said. She hardly said a word, just nodded and listened to Mr. Barker so very carefully. She never listened that hard to anything I said. But I made sure I didn't interrupt since she seemed so interested.

Surely my daddy hadn't talked such hot-air baloney. But I guessed he had a bad temper from what Mama and Doc had said. And a drinker. That was terrible news. But I tried to explain it away. Seemed like all the adults I ever saw Mama socializing with were rattling ice in cocktails before dinner. So what then? How much did Mr. Barker drink anyway? I checked his whiskey glass. Empty. Had that been his second or third?

I listened to Mr. Barker's drone. Sounded steady, no fuzzy sliding *s*'s to his speech yet. He seemed very in control. I wondered if that's what Mama liked about him. Seemed my daddy had been sort of unpredictable, definitely scary if you sassed him. I think that's one of the things I'd like to change about the world when I grow up. Just because a husband or father is the "man of the house" shouldn't give him the right to flatten someone when they talk back—wife, child, or dog, for that matter.

I went back to analyzing Mr. Barker. As far as looks, he was pretty decent. He definitely didn't have that belly-over-the-belt thing most men his age had. In fact, he kind of had a Cary Grant look to him—dark, slicked hair, dimpled chin, tall, lean, and well dressed. The creases in his linen pants looked straight and sharp enough to cut paper. But his face didn't have the amused twinkle to it that Grant had in all his movies. Mr. Barker's was dead earnest, and, I don't know, the way he looked through me felt like he'd sized me up and thrown me out all at the same time.

It was Mama's voice dropping to soft that made me tune in to what was going on. "That's right, in the rose bushes . . . all scratched up, dirty as can be . . . I just don't know how to manage her these days. . . ."

I forced myself to keep eating and not fidget with my bandages.

"She just needs a stronger hand than you like to give, Grace," he boomed, oblivious to Mama's quiet tone. "That's obvious."

"I don't know if that's it exactly," Mama said slowly. "I worry that she spends too much time here with Doc and Edna. They're wonderful help, but she should probably be playing with children her own age."

I looked up at Mama and shook my head. I liked being with Doc and Edna.

She frowned at me and turned her eyes back to Mr. Barker, as if he knew everything.

He tipped his chair back, looking mighty pleased. "You ought to bring her to the club, Grace. That's the place for her to meet the right kind of children." He thought a moment. "In fact, my sister is keeping her husband's niece this summer. Her parents are taking a cruise around the Greek isles for six weeks. Great little gal. Now she'd be a good influence on Alice. How old is she?"

I jumped in, "Eleven come October. But I don't much like children my own age, Mr. Barker. I'm fine staying here, really. Doc's keeping me busy on the roses."

He didn't even glance my way. "Nearly eleven, hmmmm. I think Bridget is twelve. Maybe thirteen. Well, she'll do it for me as a favor. She has excellent manners, is already a looker, and dresses right—a real little lady. She knows how to play a good game of tennis, too. You've probably seen her on the court. She just won the junior tournament." Mr. Barker pressed his finger-tips together. "I'll call Barb tonight and see about set-ting up a tennis date. You'll see. Good influence is what Alice needs to straighten up and fly right. Why don't we take our coffee out on the porch."

And with that he pulled out Mama's chair and herded her away from me.

CHAPTER EIGHT

life is long, child

F orty-love."

Another tennis ball whizzed by, *twanging* off the corner lines, a perfect ace.

"My game. My set."

My nightmare. That was the second set that Mr. Barker's sister's niece had won without my getting a single point. Not a single one. I counted myself lucky to have returned a couple of balls. I knew this would be a disaster. I'd told Mama. I'd told Edna. I'd told Doc. I was a terrible tennis player, and this was a terrible idea.

Doc was the only one who'd been honest about it. Both Mama and Edna said it'd be a lot of fun, nice to be with a girl my own age. I guess grown-up women get it stuck in their heads that girls have to be with girls or they grow warts or something. Doc, on the other hand, knew how spastic I was. Plus, he considered country-club sports a waste of time. "Well, it'll be fast. Life is long, child, and this tennis game is only a split second of it. You'll see."

He'd been right about it being fast at least. Within thirty minutes I'd been trounced 6-0, 6-0. But I have to say, that half hour felt like a week's worth of humiliation.

"You need some lessons," said my torturer as she came up to the net. "I could teach you."

Doc had warned me to mind my manners since this had been Mama's idea. I felt like telling Bridget to take a hike, but I swallowed instead and said, "That'd be great." I whipped out a big smile from my bag of keep-'em-happy tricks.

Bridget cocked her head to make her honey-colored ponytail do an *I Dream of Jeannie* swoosh. She was cover-girl perfect, no zits, the beginnings of a figure, big brown eyes, and a perky openness about her face. Sure to be prom queen someday. I couldn't decide whether to hate her or desperately try to be her friend so that some of that perfection might rub off on me.

"Let's get something to eat at the snack bar," I suggested. "Mama said I could treat."

"Neat."

My mouth watered over the selection of Twinkies,

Hostess Cup Cakes, Ho Hos, and candy bars. Bridget wrinkled her nose. "I'll just have lemonade. I'm watching my weight."

"Why?" I asked through a mouthful of Three Musketeers. "You look great."

She stared at me as if I was from another planet. "You better be careful, too, if you want to look like Twiggy."

"Twiggy?" The odd name sounded vaguely familiar.

Bridget rolled her eyes. "Do they keep you locked up in a barn or something? You need help, kiddo. Twiggy, as in THE fashion model of all time. The face of 1966. The model who gets $240 an hour for a photo session." She flung her arms out and did a knock-kneed pose, and then I did remember seeing a gangly, short-haired blond in a bunch of my mother's fashion magazines.

"Oh, right!"

"Well, she's five feet six inches and weighs ninety-one pounds, and her measurements are 31-22-32. I don't know if I can be that great looking, but I'm going to try. I want to be just like her or Billie Jean King before I get married and have three children—all girls I hope. Boys aren't good for anything until they're boyfriend material. I might even cut my hair, so it's bobbed like Twiggy's."

"Oh no," I gulped. "Don't cut your hair—it's so beautiful, like Rapunzel's." I blushed. Rapunzel. Did I sound like a baby, or what?

"Really?" Bridget pulled her hand down along her

ponytail to make it swing again. "Thanks." She smiled.

We were friends.

"You know, you could straighten out that hair of yours if you just slept with a roller, like I do," she said. "I pull it up on top of my head with a rubber band and roll it with one big orange-juice can."

How weird was that? But I nodded.

"I'll come over and show you someday. Wanna play later this week?"

Not really, but I nodded again and said, "Okay. Are you sure you don't mind? I mean, I'm not any good."

"That's okay. It'll be good for my game to teach a total beginner. And by the end of the summer, you might even win a game against me." Bridget grinned. "But don't expect a whole set. I'm going to London to play in Wimbledon someday. Just like Billy Jean. And I'll send you a ticket, so you can come cheer me on."

"Sure," I said. "Is Billy Jean really good?"

"She just won Wimbledon for the third year in a row, dummy. Don't you know anything? I'd have thought that your mother would have filled you in on Billie Jean King and Wimbledon, at least. She's a big tennis player, isn't she?"

Mama. I hadn't even thought that far. If I knew something about tennis, maybe we'd have more to talk about.

I straightened up, suddenly very interested. "I just hadn't asked her, that's all."

Bridget put her hand on my shoulder. "You don't have to lie to me, kiddo. I know how it is. Grown-ups just can't be bothered, can they? It's the generation gap. They can't remember what it's like to be young. And all they care about is keeping up with the Joneses and buying the latest car and kitchen appliances. My parents couldn't wait to dump me here with Aunt Barbara." She started singing in a whiny voice, imitating someone she'd listened to on the radio: "How does it feel/to be on your own . . ."

I had no idea what she was talking about, but it made me uneasy, like she knew something I didn't. "Mama's not like that, she's just . . . busy . . . or lonely . . . or worried . . . or something."

Bridget laughed, a nasally giggle I didn't like. "Mama? You still call her Mama? I sure have my work cut out for me."

CHAPTER NINE

we can be a team

S o how was that tennis date, honey bunch?" Edna asked, sliding in beside me at lunch the next day.

"Okay, I guess," I said slowly, trying to weigh Doc's reaction as I spoke. I knew he'd disapprove of my spending more time on the tennis court. "Better than I thought. I mean, she's really good and all—she creamed me. But she was neighborly enough about it." Cautiously I added, "She wants to play again on Friday, and I think I'll go."

"Well, now, that's fine news," said Edna. "Why don't you invite her back to lunch afterward?"

Doc dropped his fork with a bang. "You going to encourage this, Edna?" The morning had been a sizzler, and Doc's temper matched the temperature.

Edna ignored him. "I'll make a nice shrimp salad. And I bet Mr. McKenzie will have some sweet white corn for us by then. Don't you think, Mr. McKenzie?"

He *humpfed* and dug back into his lunch. "That's only if I beat that GD groundhog to it."

Edna kept talking, "Yes, that's fine, Alice. You haven't had many girls over here for lunch. I always loved cooking for a passel of girls. They appreciate good cooking. Why, your mama used to have flocks of girls over here all the time. Giggling and gossiping. I had a time listening to them and not giggling myself."

"Watch out or she'll turn out just like her mama," Doc mumbled.

Edna missed it, but I heard him. "What'd be wrong with that?" I asked hotly. Did he have to put Mama down *all* the time?

Doc raised his eyebrow and pointed his fork at me. "You know well enough why. I told you. Do you listen? She's so busy worrying over her clothes and tennis she doesn't pay any attention to the important things. You'd think she was one of those idiot hippies, one of them flower children screaming about free love and living in communes. They just don't want any responsibility. Like alley cats leaving behind their kittens. She don't care about you."

Edna gasped. I felt sick. Through the thunder in my ears, I heard her say in a faraway voice, "Mr. McKenzie, for shame. I'd never figured you for cruel before."

Doc dropped his head. I couldn't say anything. I could hardly breathe. "You tell this child you didn't mean it. He didn't mean it, honey lamb."

"Mean what?"

Now we all went silent and ash-faced. Mama was standing at the door.

I looked at Edna. I looked at Doc. This was a great chance for revenge, to repay Doc for what he'd just said. I opened my mouth to get him. Then I snapped it shut again. Who'd I eat lunch with if she fired him? And what if she got mad at me for talking about her?

"Oh, don't worry about it, Mama. I mean *Mother*. I was just pestering him with questions, and he said he was good and tired of it. That's okay. I know he didn't mean it." But I wasn't above giving him a little kick. "Doc wouldn't ever say anything to hurt me on purpose, would you, Doc?"

He shifted and growled, "No, I wouldn't."

Mama looked from him to me to Edna.

Uh-oh, I thought, *she's not buying it.*

But her question let me breathe again.

"*Mother*? When did she start calling me *Mother*?"

Edna spotted the save. She got up quickly and cleared her place. "She's growing up fast, Miss Grace. All of a sudden." She retreated to the sink, like she didn't belong at our table anymore. Doc did the same thing, tipping his hat as he escaped out the door. "Afternoon, Miss Grace."

"Mother?" She asked me again with a look of horror on her face.

"You don't like that? Bridget told me I sounded

like a baby saying 'Mama.'"

"Lord, no, that's what I called *my* mother. You can call me Mama a little longer, can't you, sugar?" She held her arms out for a hug, and I threw myself into them.

"I'll call you Mama forever," I said, thinking *just as long as you promise to love me forever.*

"Thank goodness, that's settled," she chirped. "I could feel a whole set of wrinkles and a head of gray hair coming on with that *Mother* business."

She plopped us down on the bench. "So tell me about tennis."

I told her. Her laugh twittered through the kitchen, and I noticed Edna slip into the pantry and disappear. "6-0, 6-0. That is pretty awful. But if Bridget teaches you to play better, maybe you and I could be a doubles team. How about that?"

My heart thumped happy. "That'd be groovy!"

"Groovy?" Mama laughed again. "I guess that's what I get for setting you up with a budding teenager. But you know what, Ally? Mr. Barker said Bridget really liked you. Guess she's been lonely down here, away from her friends and home. Thanks for being nice to her, sweet pea. That made Mr. Barker happy. You know . . ." she began to pull her words out, the way parents do when what they're saying is a big deal, but they're trying to make it seem not so. "He and I are going to spend Saturday with his grandmother. He's got all the signs of getting serious. What did you think of him?"

I knew this was dangerous territory. "Weeelll," I stalled. "He's okay looking."

Mama nodded and smiled. "He is a bit of a dreamboat, isn't he?"

"And he eats real nice."

She laughed. "Well, he should have good manners coming from his family. He has a Virginia governor and a U.S. congressman in his family tree, you know."

"Is that good?"

"Some people think so."

I wasn't sure I liked the tone of her voice. I wasn't sure how I felt about him yet, and she sounded like she'd made up her mind. Was she thinking of marrying him? It was hard enough to get her attention as it was. "Don't you think he's a little . . . well . . . bossy, Mama?"

"Bossy?" she frowned. "No, he just seems like a strong man to me. Solid, reliable, a leader. No wild, unpredictable dreams." She paused and a hint of worry slid across her face. "Did he seem bossy?"

"Kind of."

She disappeared in thought and stood up, patting me on the head. "Go on outside and play, honey. I'm heading to the beauty parlor. Mary Beth said I'd look pretty with some of those frosting streaks they're putting in her hair, and I thought I'd try it. What do you think?"

But she had left the room before I could answer.

CHAPTER TEN

nature will always give you comfort

Doc was out in the cornfield. I could hear him rustling through it. I stepped over a couple of stalks that had been mauled by the groundhog and entered the rows, swallowed up in tall green. By September, the stalks would be withered and yellow and teetering, done in by a summer of heat and their work of pushing out ears of corn. But now they were lush and beautiful, reaching up strong toward the sun. You could almost see them grow. Standing quiet among them, I could feel the power that made the earth an urgently living thing. I sucked in the scent of turned-up, baking ground. I ran my fingers down along the wide, plumelike leaves, feeling their cool smoothness, as polished and perfect as marble sculpture. I pulled out some of the golden silk that cascaded out of the ears of corn and tickled it along my face, awed by its softness. Lord, the world was an amazing place.

"I swear there's a gardener in you, Alice."

I jumped. How in the world did that creaky, old fart of a man sneak up on me like that? "I'm mad at you, Doc." I know I wasn't supposed to talk to an adult like that, but if we were friends, really friends, I should be able to be honest.

He look startled, then nodded. "I bet you are. Should be, too. I'm just turning into a cranky old man, Alice."

"How old are you anyway?"

He gave me one of his smiles that pushed around his wrinkles in a nice way. "About two thousand and eight."

"Naw, really. How old are you?"

"Oh, all right. Two thousand and four." He turned and shuffled back out of the cornrows to his wheelbarrow. He crashed down into it and started fanning himself with his hat. "Gonna be another scorcher," he mumbled, looking up at the hazy, humid sky. We hadn't seen blue, real blue, for two weeks now. Even the catbird had given up singing; it'd gotten so hot.

I squished in the wheelbarrow beside him. "Doc?"

"Hmmm?"

"You didn't mean what you said, did you?"

He took a deep breath and I held mine, waiting.

"No, Alice. Your mother loves you. She just doesn't

do right by you, or her mother, or this house, or herself." He stared off and added gruffly, "And that's the funny thing about love. It's why I always spooked away from it. Messy, trips a man up. When you see someone you care for being hurt, you get protective-like. Understand?"

For a few moments, I didn't. Then I got it. Doc was talking about me. I hugged his arm.

He shrugged and blew his nose. But I knew what he felt. Without his knowing it, Doc taught me something right then and there. Maybe he did have a little mean in him, or maybe it was just he'd gotten so old he couldn't see anything but black and white, no colors or shades in between. Whatever it was, he fought against it. And it's the trying that *really* matters. You can't have your whole opinion of someone wrapped up in a bad moment. Give a person like Doc long enough and he might just say something wonderful.

"Listen, never mind what I think about tennis," Doc went on. "Probably good for you to know about it. Your mama loves the game, and you need to get close to your mama."

"But I thought you thought country-club sports were foolish."

"Still do. But maybe it's just because I never was lucky enough to have the chance to play them."

"Well, I wish you'd make up your mind." How was I supposed to know what to do if he said one thing one day and another thing the next?

Doc snorted a laugh. "Here's the thing about adults, child. We try to have the right answers, but sometimes answers change from one day to the next because of circumstances.

"What are circumstances?"

He thought a spell, trying to figure how to explain things easy.

"It's like spring weather, Alice. The earth's mood changes, right as you're trying to use it to grow seedlings. So you've got to react to it. On warm, clear days, you put those seedlings out in the sun, right?"

"Right."

"But if there's the threat of a late frost, you've gotta pull them back inside again. Right?"

"Right. So?"

He sighed. "Never mind. Play tennis. Just don't forget what it feels like to stand in the corn or to bring in a basket of roses you've grown. No matter what's wrong in your life, if you can make flowers grow or stand still in nature, you'll find comfort. That's who you really are, child. Deep down, that's your mother, too. She just lost it in trying to be what men think they want. Who's after her now?"

"Mr. Barker."

"William Barker?"

"I think so. She called him Bill."

Doc stuck out his lower lip and nodded in grudging approval. "Well, that might be good. Been on the town council for a couple terms. Heard in the hardware store that he was going to run for lieutenant governor next election. Probably campaigning already. Lawyer. Lots of acreage in the family. Alice, that might be the best thing for you. A stepdaddy like that."

I jumped up out of the wheelbarrow. "I don't want any stepdaddy, Doc. Why does she have to marry anyone at all?"

He looked at me hard. "Well, to my way of thinking, she doesn't have to. But your mother's a man's woman. She don't trust herself enough to stand on her own. Now Miss Margaret could have. But Miss Grace don't. You're going to end up with a stepdaddy sooner or later. I'm surprised it's taken this long, if you want to know the truth of it. Anyway, better to have a good provider."

"Why can't she be a provider?"

"She threw away her education for your daddy, that's why. She don't know how to earn a living."

Doc's face got a glazed look to it, and he started squeezing his left arm, like he'd hit his funny bone or something. "Enough. Lord, you do ask questions, child." He patted my back. "Scoot up to the house and get me some water, will you, Alice?"

I scooted, glad we were right with each other again. When I got back, Doc had lain down flat in the wheelbarrow and was snoring like a hound dog. His mouth was wide open, and his dentures had slipped off his gums. No wonder he made such a racket when he chewed. I covered his face with his straw hat, so he wouldn't suck in any gnats.

I skipped back toward the house to get my tennis racket and hit some balls against the garage door, the way Bridget had told me to practice. If I was going to keep playing with her, I needed to figure out how to stop looking like a horse's behind on the court.

Besides, I had a goal now. Mama had said if I learned to play, we might could be a doubles team. As I whacked the ball, I reminded myself not to get too excited. Mama had made promises before she didn't keep for some reason or another. But maybe . . . just maybe . . . this time would be different.

CHAPTER ELEVEN

talking about parents causes headaches

You just toss it into the air and then . . ." Bridget swung her racket back and up in a graceful, quick arc. "Slam it!" Her ball sailed over the net to bounce in the corner of the serving square. "Now you go."

I reached into the basket of balls. That was about the twentieth time she'd shown me how to serve. I hadn't gotten one in the square yet.

"Just visualize it going in the sweet spot," said Bridget. She'd told me her mother took yoga, some eastern mysticism thing where she tried to twist her body into a pretzel, and her instructor talked about picturing goals. "If you visualize the ball going in, your mind will tell your body to do it. Promise."

I squeezed my eyes closed. I imagined the ball in my hand floating up over my head and my racket hitting it straight and true for an ace in the corner.

I threw the ball up.

I swung.

My racket hit—and . . .

My ball swerved to the left, *twanging* the fence.

"Try again. *See* it first."

That ball hit the net. The next one piddled to a stop on my side of the court. I completely missed the third and banged my leg with the wooden racket instead.

I hadn't visualized any of that.

When the whole basket was empty and all the balls lay in the alley or the outside of the fence, Bridget shook her head. "Why don't we just volley for a while?"

"Okay." That sounded much better.

I actually managed to bat the ball back and forth a little. I didn't even care that she was hitting soft, right to me, like you would to a total doofus. "So what's your mother like?" I asked as I lobbed a loopy ball at her.

Bridget zinged it past me on the return. "I told you: Mrs. Robinson all the way. Haven't you seen that movie, *The Graduate*?"

I certainly hadn't. It was for grown-ups. I knew that much. *Doctor Doolittle* was more my speed.

"Well, it's about a mother who acts like she's twenty instead of forty and wants center stage all the time. She even goes after one of her daughter's boyfriends. It's pretty disgusting." Bridget's returns were getting harder and zingier and madder as she talked. "My mother looks and acts a lot like Mrs. Robinson. She wears all that leopard and fake zebra stuff. Very chic, according to *Vogue*. Does her shopping in the city, darling, at Saks."

Bridget's father was an investment banker. They lived just outside New York City, in a New Jersey suburb. The geography alone put me in awe of her. She'd been to three Broadway musicals.

"She does keep me up on things, though, I have to admit," Bridget said. She paused to whap a spinning serve at me. "She sent me *Waiting for the Sun*, Jim Morrison and the Doors' latest album, and she promised to take me to see *Hair* when she gets back."

While Bridget talked, a miracle happened. She missed my return!

"Hey! Hey!" I started to jump up and down. "Hey! I won a point!"

But she didn't seem interested. "Let's stop now, okay? Talking about my parents gives me a sick headache." And she walked off the court.

Back home, Edna made a big fuss over Bridget.

"Mighty glad to have you here today, Miss Bridget. Alice has told us so much about you. Awful nice of you to teach her tennis."

"You can just call me Bridget," said Bridget as she sat down at the table. She rolled her eyes at me.

I tilted my head, silently asking what's up? But she waved me off when Edna turned away.

The table was set with linen placemats, and Edna had even pulled out the long silver spoons for ice tea. There were little mint leaves, fresh from the garden, in the iced glasses, just the way she did things for Mama.

Doc stomped into the kitchen. He hung his straw hat by the door, and I jumped up to take his hand. Doc's manners were usually decent, but his mood might not be, and he definitely wasn't all that friendly with strangers.

"Doc," I looked up into his gnarly, old face with a help-me-out-here smile. "This is my friend, Bridget. Mr. Barker's sister's niece. Remember?" I turned to Bridget. "Bridget, this is Doc. He's the one who makes the roses grow."

Doc stood up taller. He said hello instead of grunting his greeting. Bridget smiled prettily at him. But when he slumped down across the table from her, her smile faded. I couldn't figure it out. I sniffed the air. He didn't smell bad or anything. I have to admit that sometimes he did stink when he'd been using horse manure to fertilize things. He claimed it made his roses zoom. But today he smelled fine.

Edna proudly put down a platter of shrimp salad. We hardly ever had it, being in the middle of the state, way away from the coast. I knew Edna had to prerequest the shrimp at the grocery store and had asked Mama for extra spending money. It was a special treat. I smiled my thanks at her. It really was a pretty sight: the pink shrimp with the green celery and scallions were arranged on watercress and ringed by wedges of Doc's sweet, tender tomatoes. I knew darn well that it'd been Edna, her cooking and her clever arrangement of food that had made my grandmother a big-time hostess in the county. I wondered if the famous Miss Margaret even knew how to boil an egg.

Edna spooned out Bridget's helping and added a steaming ear of sweet corn, just picked and shucked that morning. Bridget squirmed back in her seat, like she'd been given liver for dinner.

The rest of us dug in. Bridget pushed her shrimp around to the edges of her plate, here and there, making it look like she had eaten some of it. I knew that trick.

"Edna," Doc said, after inhaling his portions, "that was about the most wonderful lunch I've had."

"Why, thank you, Mr. McKenzie."

He continued wiping his mouth, the cloth scraping along his shaved, but already bristly, face. "Alice should ask such nice young ladies to lunch more . . ." Doc stopped abruptly. He'd just noticed Bridget's plate.

I talked fast to save Edna's feelings and to stop the insult I knew Doc would feel at her not touching his precious sun-ripe tomatoes. "She never eats much of anything, Doc. She wants to look like Twiggy."

Doc scowled.

"Who's Twiggy?" Edna asked, trying to keep things civilized.

"A British fashion model," answered Bridget. "I'm sure she doesn't show up in any of the magazines *you* might read."

I looked nervously from Edna to Doc. Edna's face had gone blank, a seamless mask. Doc's was a thunderclap.

"Actually," Bridget continued, "I'm not dieting today, Alice. I just prefer fresh, iced shrimp, you know, the kind they bring at restaurants as appetizers with horseradish and cocktail sauce." Only then did she notice Edna's hurt expression. "No offense, Edna."

"None taken, miss," Edna said quietly, in a voice she used when answering our phone for Mama. She stood up from the table stiffly and carried away the plates. "I hope you like lemon meringue pie, though."

Wow. Edna had gone all out. "This is the best," I reassured Bridget.

I avoided Doc's glare.

Every bite of my piece of pie melted sweet and tart and creamy. I knew how long Edna'd stood and beaten those egg whites in such summer heat to get the meringue stiff and fluffy at the same time. I owed her a big hug.

I was having such a good time eating that pie, I'd forgotten to keep an eye on Bridget.

She'd scraped out the filling and meringue, leaving

the shell still a perfect-standing wedge.

Edna looked stricken.

"Can we be excused now, Alice?" Bridget was saying. She ignored Edna and Doc when she asked.

Doc half stood with that look he got chasing the GD groundhog all over his face. Instantly, Edna reached over and put her hand over his, whispering. "It's all right, Percy. It's not worth it. But thank you all the same." Doc plopped back down and growled at his plate. Edna squeezed his hand before withdrawing hers.

Bridget's eyes got as big as golf balls.

"Let's go." I popped up. "Thanks, Edna. That was wonderful. See ya later, Doc."

I hustled Bridget up to my room.

She closed the door with her back and stood there, her mouth hanging open. "Did you see that?"

"What?"

"She held his hand."

"No, she didn't, she just reached over to keep Doc from yelling at you. And so what if she had?"

Bridget stayed pinned to the door. "Alice, you are so blind. A Negro woman held a white man's hand in your kitchen. Father says the whole reason they're getting so militant is that mealymouthed liberals like the Kennedys and Lyndon Johnson encouraged them."

"What do you mean by militant?"

She almost shouted back at me, "Militant. Militant. Saying 'if you don't give us what we want, we'll take it by force.' Don't you know about all the trouble some of them are causing? How dangerous those Black Panthers are with their black-gloved fists and Afros? Crowds of blacks burned half of Newark last summer. A couple dozen people died. This spring they tore up all the stores after King was shot. They rolled over cars and set them on fire. They had guns and shot at police in Harlem. It took days to stop it. That rioting wasn't all that far from where I live.

"Right before I got shipped down here, Father and Mother took me to an Italian restaurant in Newark as a 'special treat.'" She held up her fingers and made fake quotation marks in the air as she said the last two words. "I'll say it was a special treat. We got lost in the wrong end of town. Two Negroes threw beer bottles at our car and shouted obscenities at us because we were white 'honkies.'"

"But this is Doc and Edna," I interrupted. I knew about all the rioting. Who didn't? The TV news played hours of it. Edna didn't have anything to do with that. I'd never even connected Edna with those angry mobs before. And she and Doc were friends. How could they not be—they'd worked together for forever.

Bridget took in a breath to keep going but stopped as if a new thought—a more basic problem—tripped her up. "And I can't believe you eat lunch with the help. Does your mother?"

I looked at her a moment, and my answer was full of

an icky recognition. "No," I said slowly. I never had seen Mama sit down with Edna and Doc, now that Bridget mentioned it. Not even when she gave them their Christmas presents.

"Well, that's good, at least. Aunt Barbara's brother—that Mr. Barker your mother's so interested in—wouldn't like it. Let's just eat lunch at the club from now on, okay?"

"Okay," I answered grudgingly. "I guess so." I figured it was better anyway—given the look on Doc's face, he might have tried to paddle Bridget's bottom with a shovel the next time he saw her.

CHAPTER TWELVE

*attitudes are slower
to change than law*

Next morning, I made good with Edna first. She'd
be easy. With Doc, I'd have to test things out, like sticking your toes in a pool before deciding whether it's too
cold to jump in. With Edna, I could just walk right up
and speak my mind.

I found her in the kitchen and hugged her. "I'm sorry
about yesterday, Edna," I said into her apron.

She hugged me back. "That wasn't you, Alice. I was
mighty proud of how you didn't start talking like her. I
always told my children, if it doesn't sound good coming
out of your friend's mouth, it's not going to sound any
better coming out of yours. Trash talk is trash talk."

"I think she's kind of . . . spoiled, I guess."

"You guess right. Remember, Alice, you can't pick family, but you pick your friends. And your friends say something about you."

"But Mama wants me to be friends with Bridget. Because of that Mr. Barker."

Edna pressed her lips together and then said, "Sometimes the Lord sends conundrums that take us a while to figure out. Shoo now; I've got peaches to can."

I paused at the door. "Thank you, Edna. And for the lunch, too. It was really good."

"You're welcome, baby. G'on now."

I found Doc in the roses. He was working on getting them perfect for Mama's party, coming in three weeks. He was pruning and deadheading to force them to bloom on that very day. Mama had set the party—as her mother always did—for Labor Day weekend, a kind of farewell to summer.

We would all be ready to kiss that sticky-hot summer good-bye. As far as the party theme goes, she had perfect timing. But it was terrible timing for roses. End of September would have been much better. By then the air would be cool, the sun would stop simmering, and the roses would be at their best. May, June, September, and October—those were the best months for roses.

But Mama never kept track of things like that. And no matter how much she resented Doc, she knew he could make them bloom when he wanted to.

It was a pretty amazing trick. Most rosebushes in late August are wilted, limp, and naked from black spot. Not ours. Doc whipped those roses into bloom for Mama's party. If each bush pushed out twenty blossoms, there'd be close to twenty-five hundred rose blooms total, making flower rainbows throughout the yard.

"Those roses are going to look great, Doc. Just like always. Need any help?"

No answer.

So we were going to go through this dance again. I sighed. "Pruning, Doc?"

Silence.

"Roses sure are hard work, Doc."

Silence.

I sat down in the wheelbarrow and scratched my arm. I only had one scab left from the rose attack weeks before where the dig had been deep. It was miserable hot, and sweat was making it scream for a scratch, especially since it was peeling up at the end, ready to shed.

"Quit picking at that scab, Alice. You'll give yourself bad scars."

Eureka. He'd spoken.

"How do you know about scars and stuff, Doc?"

He cut off several blown-out blooms. Then he turned around and leaned down toward me. "I'm going to tell you how I learned. You may not like it. You ready?"

I tucked my knees up under my chin, like you do

when watching a scary movie. "Ready," I said.

"You know I run off to the Great War, World War One."

"Why'd you do that, Doc?'

"Never mind now." He frowned down at me. "You gonna listen?"

"Yes, sir. Sorry." Next time I felt a question coming, I'd pinch myself to stop it.

"The Great War was fought in trenches, like long, unending graves. They teach you that in school?"

"No, sir. Not yet."

"Well, it was. All the kings and queens and dukes and hoity-toity aristocrats of Europe decided they wanted what each other had. They dug in for a fight. Nasty fight. They had no idea what they were going to bring on themselves, how good their new guns were at blowing up boys into bits and pieces. Well, that's how I learned about scars and scabs and amputations and dying—fishing broken bodies out of the trenches and driving them to the hospital. Nothing like the hospitals that you know. Just tents where boys screamed and nurses tried their hardest to ease their last moments."

He paused, and I noticed his old eyes were bleary.

"In those long ditches, regiments got mixed together. I ended up driving ambulances for the medics from England and France as well as America. Even helped a Turk one day. Out there on the battlefield when boys cry and clutch at your ankles as you walk past, you just pick them up. If you're human, anyway."

I started to say that it sounded pretty awful, but he waved me off.

"Now, here's the part I really wanted to tell you. The man I learned the most from was a dark-skinned fellow from India. He'd been studying in England to become a doctor. When the war broke out, he left schooling and joined the British to help in the hospitals. The way he bandaged boys and splinted their legs was better than any of the other medics. Better than a lot of doctors. He'd studied surgery. He should have been operating— not dodging bullets to pick up the injured off the ground."

"Well, why wasn't he?" I asked.

Doc looked at me hard. "For the same reason your fancy friend was so rude to Edna yesterday."

I tried to find the answer in his face but couldn't. So I rummaged through what Bridget had said in my room. I found it there. "She thinks she's better than Edna, doesn't she?"

"Bingo." Doc crossed his arms across his chest. "The British looked down on the Indians. Back then, India was a British colony. Indians were mostly servants to the Brits. During the war, a lot of the officers didn't want a dark man as their doctor. So my friend had to be a medic on an ambulance instead. What do you think of that? And what do you think about some spoiled rotten brat talking down to a woman who had gone to that much trouble to make her a nice lunch?"

Not much. I hung my head and fought back embarrassed tears. Even though I hadn't talked like Bridget and didn't think like she did, I hadn't corrected her either. I'd stood by and let her hurt Edna.

"Doc?"

He grunted his "What?"

I was swimming in the mess of questions and confusing emotions that yesterday had brought out. "Are you and Edna in love?"

"What? Is that what that idiot child . . . well . . ." He interrupted himself with a snort. "That figures." Then he started laughing, a big guffawing, denture-rattling hee-haw. "I bet . . ." He gasped for air. "I bet that about curled her hair." Ha-ha-ha-ha.

I couldn't laugh, though. "Doc, she pretty much said Negroes are dangerous."

Doc stopped laughing abruptly. "What do you think?"

"Well, I know Edna isn't; her family isn't. But all the riots on TV are pretty scary."

He nodded. "Yes, they are."

"Why are they happening, Doc?"

Doc motioned for me to get up, and he sat and pulled me on his knee. "You know, one of Edna's sons worked with Martin Luther King, Jr. Joined him right after the Reverend spoke here at the university, back in 1963. Did you know that? Edna's mighty proud on it."

I didn't know. But it made sense given Edna's gentleness. I knew Reverend King had preached "nonviolence," sitting down at the table with one another to talk out disagreements, no matter what color we are.

"King's people tried to change the world with sit-ins and peaceful marches. And cracker whites in Alabama answered them with fire hoses and dogs and jail time. But King and his people kept at it. They got some important things changed. Colored folks can sit and eat lunch at restaurants and ride anywhere they darn well please on buses. Black and white children are going to school together so they have equal education. It's law, been that way for a number of years now.

"But attitudes are slower to change. And then Reverend King got killed this spring. Race riots started for real. Now some of their leaders are calling for a separate black nation, no matter what they have to do to get it. I don't agree with that. Scares me, too. Crowds get out of hand. Hurt more than stores—women, children. . . ." He stopped and looked at me.

"Lawlessness ain't no good answer, ever. The trouble in the cities is going to spread if they keep at it. I even heard tell that one of the Virginia students got his tires slashed in town the other day because he was out trying to encourage some high school Negroes to apply to the university. Dang fools. No, sir. Fighting just brings on more hatred. Look at the First World War—'the war to end all wars', they said. Twenty years later the very same people were at it again. But I can see that Negroes—" he interrupted himself. "They want to be called Blacks now, I need to try to remember. Anyway, they're tired of waiting, waiting to get what the constitution and human decency say they should have—being treated the same as us. Can't say as how I blame them. Can you?"

I shook my head no. We both sat silently for a few minutes. Then I said, "Thanks for explaining stuff to me."

He grunted his "You're welcome," pleased, I think. It seemed real important to him that I listen to it all.

"You know the major regret I have about my life?" Doc asked.

"That you can't get rid of the GD groundhog?"

"No, child." He rubbed his forehead. "It's that I didn't have the guts to tell off the British for my friend. His name was Indra." He went on, his voice hoarse, "He died. A mortar shell landed near him while we were getting the wounded off the field. He was last in line at the hospital I suspect because of his skin. His wounds were worse. He was bleeding bad but not from the gut, not from the chest. The gut and the chest are what kill you. If they'd taken him first, they probably could have patched him up. But instead, he bled to death while he waited. Maybe if I had made a bigger stink . . . Well, at least I had the spine to hold his hand and talk to him while he died."

Doc stood up, dumping me into the wheelbarrow, and wiped his eyes.

"See, what really matters, Alice, is believing in what you know is right, in your gut, no matter what friends, or superior officers, or country-club rules say. The world is changing fast. Never seen anything like the last few years. And the change will be good. But there's a lot of anger and lashing-out right now. You gotta keep your head, Alice. Stand up for yourself and what you know is right. Grown people come to believe a lot of foolish things because of money, status, old prejudices that their class of people tells them are proper. They're afraid of losing their place at the top of the hill. But the more they fight change, the harder change is going to kick—the bloodier it's going to be in coming.

"Life is going to test you that way, Alice. Lunch yesterday was just the beginning. And how you deal with those tests is the measure of what kind of person you are."

He shaded his eyes with his hand and looked off in the distance. He dropped his hand and mumbled, "I failed my test, Alice. I worry that your mama is failing hers. Don't you."

I watched him walk away, slow and sad, up toward the shade trees, and I worried. Worried about trying to understand him, worried about this test he talked about. It probably was a good thing I didn't know then that the biggest test of my life was gathering speed, heading right for me, like a hundred-mile-per-hour hurricane toward the Outer Banks. If I had known, I might have tried to fit down the groundhog's tunnel to hide.

CHAPTER THIRTEEN

you've got a thinker inside you

Three August weeks passed in a haze of 100-plus humidity and tennis-court humiliation. Bridget kept asking me, so I kept going—working on learning the game, working on avoiding the subject of Edna and Doc since it seemed to cause trouble between us. I just figured the way she felt about Edna was her bad spot. Everyone had one. I know that wasn't exactly standing up for what I knew was right. But Mama wanted me to play with her. Mr. Barker wanted me to play with her. And I was learning a lot about tennis—Mama's favorite subject—from playing with her. It was a definite conundrum, just like Edna had said.

Before I knew it, it was the Monday before the party.

By 8:00 A.M., Edna was already polishing every bit of silver in the house. Bud vases, Jefferson bowls and cups, platters, serving dishes, and silverware were laid out aglistening across the dining-room table. The room reeked of the polish's bitter metallic smell. I picked up an old fork that had almost all its silver rubbed off. *Eaton* was written in tiny cursive at its base. I couldn't remember which great-grandmother that name belonged to. I was just about to ask Edna when she scolded, "Now, honey bunch, don't be putting your fingerprints all over my hard work. Go find something to do in your room."

It was going to be that kind of week—stay out of the way, Alice. Don't be causing any trouble, Alice. I don't have time for that today, Alice.

I decided to go down to the creek to make a mud castle. I spent a few minutes pushing the back screen door open and shut, open and shut, trying to get its *squeeaaakk* as long and haunted-house-like as possible.

"Aaaaalice?"

Startled, I slammed the door shut hard. "Sorry, Mama." I was expecting a lecture on busting the back door.

"'Bout what?" she asked. She standing right behind me, all dressed to go into town. She had on a bright red, sleeveless, triangular-shaped dress. Very bright, very notice-me. She dropped her wallet into her shiny patent-leather handbag and snapped it closed.

"Never mind. Where you going, Mama?"

"Where are *we* going, silly. Let's go buy you a party dress. I decided last night that you should have a new one. Bet the hem of last year's would be miles above your knees, you've grown so tall. Miniskirts are terrific, but I don't want you indecent."

My heart jumped like it does when you sweep up high on a good swing. She'd noticed I'd gotten tall? We were going shopping together? Most times we ordered things from the Sears catalog.

"Really?"

"Yes, really. Go put on those nice khaki culottes I got you. Hurry."

I raced. We were in her VW Bug in ten minutes flat.

"Let's put the top down. Okay with you, old girl?" Mama said, patting the Bug's dashboard. Mama loved that car and talked to it like it was human. I suppose that's because it was the first one she'd bought for herself, all on her own.

With the car top down, my hair would be a tumbleweed by the time we got to Charlottesville. Hers would be perfect as always, held back with a white gauzy scarf. It was worth the price of tangles, though, to have the air whipping us cool on such a blistering day.

"So how's tennis going?" she shouted, so I could hear over the wind. "You still liking it?"

"Yes, ma'am." I leaned over, so she could hear me. "I'm even serving okay now. Nothing you can't return,

94

but I'm getting them in."

"That's great."

"Yesterday, Bridget and I played our last game, a kind of good-bye tournament. She's leaving tomorrow. Guess what the score was?" I didn't even wait for an answer; I was so excited about being able to impress Mama. "It was 6-2, 3-6, 6-4. Bridget won, but that was pretty good, huh?"

"Wow!" She shouted back, but because I was leaning over toward her, I heard her say more to herself than to me, "That was sweet of Bridget."

"What do you mean 'sweet'?" I asked, a suspicion forming.

Mama looked back at me startled. "I didn't say anything, honey."

But I knew better. It was like the times I'd shoved cookies in my pocket and then claimed I hadn't been doing anything hanging by the pantry.

I sat back, my pride smacked. Sweet? Did she think Bridget'd let me win those points? The thought had never occurred to me. Now I'd never know for sure. Why would Mama say that?

I stared out the window at Albemarle County's wooded hills and sun-scalded fields, now yellow and tired looking. Mama clearly didn't realize what I was thinking and said, "You'll be a tennis star yet, Alice. Why don't we try to play a game together next Saturday?"

I forgot her careless insult. This invitation was what I'd been working for all summer. "That'd be cool, Mama."

She smiled, pleased. I had to admit she was trying, too. She seemed so much happier these days. I tried to hope the reason was more me than Mr. Barker.

"Mama?"

She turned to look at me. I wanted to ask her about what Bridget had said and whether she had ever eaten lunch with Doc and Edna, at least when she was young like me. But her eyes were hidden behind her jet-black sunglasses. I wouldn't be able to read them. I hesitated.

She reached out to touch my hand and then quickly withdrew it to shift gears. "What is it, sweet pea?"

I realized that I would completely blow it by asking something controversial. "Soooo," I scrambled to come up with another thought, "is Billy Jean King your favorite tennis player?"

"My goodness. You're becoming a real tennis buff, aren't you, Alice? We're going to have such fun playing together. You know, I don't tell many people this, but I really love tennis because I love feeling myself move that fast. My body feels so much stronger, too. And I have to admit that I *love* doing drop shots that surprise my opponent—you know, winning with a clever game?" She grinned at me. "Especially when I play men." Her mischief-making look faded a little—but just a little. "I suppose I shouldn't admit that. Doesn't sound ladylike.

Ladies aren't supposed to be competitive, are we?"

"Why's that?"

She shrugged and laughed. "I don't know. Maybe that's something you girls can change. Or maybe Billy Jean King will for you. She claims to be as good as men—even demanding that she be paid as much for winning a tournament. Can you imagine?"

"You mean she's not paid the same? Why not?"

Mama laughed again. "Goodness, Alice, you ask such questions." She shook her head. "But maybe they're good questions to ask."

We came to the edge of town. As we stopped at a stoplight, two full-of-themselves University of Virginia boys whistled at Mama. She ignored them but smiled all the same. "The college boys are back in town." She was sure to get lots of whistles now.

"I'll never be as pretty as you, Mama."

"Oh, pretty is as pretty does," she said. Then she clapped her hand over her mouth. "I can't believe I said that. That's what Mother always said to me when she caught me at the mirror. I was supposed to be neat and feminine and take care of myself to be pretty, but then when I seemed like I was doing exactly what she told me to, she'd accuse me of being conceited and shallow. Ally, don't ever let me do you that way."

She pulled into a parking space on University Avenue, which edges downtown and the college grounds. She yanked up the emergency brake, turned off the motor, and twisted in her seat to face me. "You've got a pretty girl in you, Alice. You'll grow into yourself before you know it. I see a lot of Lyle in your face, and he was gorgeous. And you know what's even better?"

"What?"

"You've got a thinker inside you. That's something I never had."

"Thank you, Mama." That was about the best compliment she'd ever given me. "You really believe that?"

Mama opened her mouth to answer, but a crowd of students suddenly bustled past the car, carrying posters that read "Stop the War!" "Peace Now" and "McCarthy for President." Most of them still had cropped hair and wore button-down shirts and ties, like the university had traditionally required. But some had chin-length, straggly hair. A couple wore T-shirts with big "peace" signs on them. Their leader held a megaphone.

"Ready?" he called.

"Ready!" answered his friends.

He began chanting: "Hey, Hey, LBJ, how many kids did you kill today?"

The crowd picked up the rhyme and held up their signs.

"What's going on?" I asked, my eyes wide. This was just like TV.

Mama looked worried, but tried to hide it. "Nothing,

sweetie. Just a bunch of college kids, probably been smoking marijuana or eating acid or whatever it is that they do. The Democrats are picking their presidential candidate this week, and the college students want someone who will promise to end the war in Vietnam. I thought Virginia boys had more sense."

"But why are they shouting about President Johnson and killing kids?"

Mama had had enough of my questions, I guess. She popped out of the car and stood on the sidewalk, waiting for me. "Come on, Alice. Let's find a pretty dress for a pretty girl."

CHAPTER FOURTEEN

allowed and wanted
are two different things

We tried on a thousand dresses. Not really, but it sure felt like it. Whatever I put on made my legs look like ten-foot-long beanstalks—not in the Twiggy way at all. More like Ichabod Crane in that Halloween story. To make it worse, I was right between girls' dresses and juniors. The girls' dresses fit, but they made me look like a three-year-old. The juniors' dresses hung like a paper bag on me. I bet Bridget would look beautiful in all of them. There was one dress that was bright navy blue, with big white stars all over it that I really, really wanted. But Mama said it was disrespectful of the American flag.

Finally, we settled on an empire waist, baby-blue

eyelet dress, with red piping around the chest and short sleeves. I hated the Peter Pan collar, but it fit nicely, and Mama promised to pull the front of my hair up with a red ribbon and flip the rest with her curlers. She said she'd seen Caroline Kennedy wearing a dress cut the exact same way in a *Life* magazine spread about JFK's widow dating a Greek millionaire.

We went to lunch in one of the restaurants near the college. The fans in the high ceiling were whirling as fast as airplane propellers to keep the air moving and cool, but the place still smelled of overpercolated coffee, sweet donuts, and french fries. We slipped into a table right by the window, sitting side by side to see out. The crowd of students was now parked on the lawn near the Rotunda. They were still chanting. More people were joining them all the time. It definitely looked more like a party than a serious protest.

Mama ordered cold tomato soup and a tuna-fish salad, and I got a club sandwich, carefully pushing aside the potato chips that had gotten soaked with pickle juice. Mama stole my pickle circles and winked at me. I scootched up close to her, thrilled to be awash in her sunlight, all by myself.

"I'm having a great time, Mama. Thank you."

"Me, too, sweet pea. You know, we should . . ."

That's when a big hand rapped on the window. "Why, Miss Grace," Mr. Barker called through the glass. "Are you window dressing?" He barged through the nearby door, shouting his hellos to the owner and several other men beside him, before standing like a giant over us.

I wanted to scream, "Go away!" but Mama was already pink in the face and fidgeting with her napkin.

"Hello, Bill. What a nice surprise."

He leaned over me, smothering me with his oatmeal-colored linen coat, and laid a big sloppy, noisy smooch on Mama's cheek. "No surprise, Grace. I called the house and knew you were in town. Came looking for you."

As he straightened up, he looked down at me. "Alice," he smiled. "Why don't you let me sit there, and you and Bridget go sit at the counter? I'll treat you both to a banana split."

I hadn't even noticed Bridget standing behind him.

She held up her hand and waved, giving me a what-can-I-say smirk.

We sat down at the counter on two high swivel chairs. "I can't believe he thinks I'll eat a banana split," she groaned. "Coffee, please," she said to the waitress. "And is that apple pie any good?" She pointed to a pie overflowing with diced apples and cinnamon under a glass cake dish.

"It's the best in the county, hon'," answered the waitress. "My cousin bakes them herself." She pulled a pencil out of her teased-to-the-roof hair to write down our order.

Bridget wrinkled her nose. "I'll try it. Heat it up, though, okay?"

The waitress turned to me.

"Strawberry ice cream, please."

We both picked at our dessert. I'd lost my appetite. Bridget said the pie was too sugary and the coffee too watery.

"Since when do you drink coffee?" I asked.

"Since always. Our cook makes it for me."

My good mood had turned sour. "When do you leave anyway?" I realized my tone didn't sound too friendly, so I added quickly, "I'm going to miss you."

"Tomorrow afternoon. Aunt Barbara's coming up to visit Mother, and she's getting her hair done today for the trip. So her brother, *your* Mr. Barker, has been dragging me around all morning."

I listened to Mr. Barker's loud voice filling up the restaurant. He wasn't even talking to Mama. A crowd of men surrounded their table now. "He's not *my* Mr. Barker," I grumbled.

"Oh, you better watch yourself, Alice. He's got plans for your mother. And he's got something to give you. It's pretty, too. I picked it out."

"Really?"

She nodded and I swung myself around to watch him. I could only see a patch of Mama's red dress among the seersucker suits.

"So what are you going to do about these darn kids?"

asked one man. "Look at them out there."

The suits turned toward the window.

"Bunch of yellow bellies."

"Bill, can't you town council people pass an ordinance against 'em?"

"Heard on the radio there're so many doped-up kids on the streets at the Democratic National Convention that Chicago's mayor called out twenty-three thousand police and National Guard."

"Good idea," Mr. Barker finally spoke up. "There's nothing wrong with those college kids that a good shot with a high-pressure fire hose wouldn't cure."

The men laughed and nodded.

Mr. Barker kept preaching. "Now that we don't have to worry about that fool Kennedy boy babying them, the government can get serious about putting a stop to all this nonsense. Nixon will beat McCarthy or Humphrey easily because he has the backing of those of us who still believe in flag, God, and family. He calls us 'the silent majority.' Well, maybe we shouldn't be silent any longer." He looked to his listeners, who nodded, like they were in a trance or something.

He continued, his pause timed perfectly—long enough to get those head bobs, short enough to prevent interruptions. "Nixon won't put up with the protests. He knows that we've got to stop the Vietcong commies where they are, or they'll be right here on our doorstep, and then how'll those spoiled, ungrateful college kids feel? Bet they won't be talking about 'flower power' or sticking daisies in guardsmen's rifles then!"

"Atta, boy, Bill."

"Darn tootin'."

"I told you fellas that we need Bill Barker running this state and running it soon."

The men laughed again. One of them slapped Mr. Barker's back.

With that, they left. Mr. Barker whirled around and caught me staring at him.

"Alice," he boomed. "I almost forgot. Bridget and I have something for you. She tells me you're her best friend. I told her that you and I are friends, too. So Bridget and I got a just-because present for you."

I was totally surprised. I didn't know what to say.

Mr. Barker pulled from his breast pocket a long, thin box, wrapped up with a stiff silver ribbon.

"Jewelry. Expensive," Bridget whispered in my ear.

Mama came over to watch.

My hands shook a little as I took the box and undid the knot. Nobody had given me a present like this before. I popped open the lid. Inside was a gold-chain bracelet with a tennis racket charm attached. I caught my breath. "Thank you, Mr. Barker. It's really beautiful."

Mr. Barker straightened his bow tie and said, "It was my pleasure, Alice. Truly." He gave me an honest-to-God nice smile. Maybe he wasn't so bad after all.

"Look, Mama. It's just like your charm bracelet."

"It's gorgeous, sweetie." She looked up at Mr. Barker, whose handsome, Coppertone-tan face seemed mighty pleased with itself. "Bill, that was very generous and very thoughtful of you. It's lovely."

This time when Mr. Barker swept Mama back up under his armpit, I didn't mind so much.

"It was nothing, Grace. I just thought Alice here is seeming so ladylike, she should have something nice to wear to your party." He leaned down and tried to whisper into Mama's ear, but I don't think his voice was able to get that small. "See what I told you. I knew Bridget'd be a good influence."

I didn't care. I latched the bracelet on and watched it shine in the sun. I felt very grown up.

Bridget leaned over to cup her hand around my ear, and said, "Play your cards right, kiddo, and there'll be more of that to come. Can you dig it?"

Now a foursome, we gathered our things to go. Mr. Barker held the door for us to pass under his arm. As we spilled out onto the sidewalk, a black woman and her daughter paused in front of the door. They were dressed in their Sunday best and carried a big shopping bag. The girl looked to be about six years old. I guessed they'd been doing her very first shop for school clothes. I was so happy with the day I grinned at the little girl. She grinned back.

"Hey," I said.

"Hey," said the little girl.

"Been shopping for school?"

She nodded.

"First grade?"

"Mmhmm," she nodded again.

"First grade is great. I loved first grade. You going in for lunch?"

The little girl looked up to her mother for the answer.

"We was thinking about it, Miss," her mother said, looking at me, then Mama, then Mr. Barker. It was only then that I noticed everybody seemed frozen—even Mr. Barker in the doorway.

But I kept on jabbering, all juiced up from our shopping and the bracelet. "You should. The food's really good. They even have great pickles according to my Mama."

The little girl's mother drew in a deep breath and took her daughter's hand. "Let's go in, then, honey."

She moved forward but hesitated at the door since Mr. Barker was still half in it. "Oh, by all means," he said, sweeping his free hand toward the inside.

The mother and daughter walked in and took our seat in the window—the only table that was empty. Businessmen filled the rest.

Mr. Barker took Mama's hand and pulled her to walk several strides ahead of Bridget and me. "Remind me to not take her campaigning with us when I'm up for election," he said to Mama.

"What'd I do now?" I whispered to Bridget.

"You're such a dope, Alice. They're sitting in the front window like an advertisement to all the Negroes in town because you invited them in."

"But Doc says they're allowed to eat wherever they want to now, Bridget."

"Well, sure, they're allowed to, but *allowed* and *wanted* are two different things."

"But that mother and her little girl wanted to go in. I could tell."

"I wasn't talking about what *they* wanted. You need a brain transplant, Alice," is all she'd answer. Then she hurried up her walk so that she was a good three feet in front of me, like I had cooties or something.

CHAPTER FIFTEEN

never stand like a whipped puppy

I said a mixed-up good-bye to Bridget that afternoon. I was a little relieved that she was leaving and a little sad. It would have been nice if she could have come to Mama's big bash. She was my only friend close to my own age, and I had learned a lot from her about tennis, about music, about clothes. I realized when I was around her that I didn't know much about what kids my age were into. It was kind of fun to know.

And yet, I knew Bridget wasn't as good a friend as Doc. She could act so superior and talk down to me without explaining why. And some of the things she taught me I wasn't so sure about—like being better than Edna just because she was our cook and a Negro. Edna was like family, really, and one of the wisest people I knew. Also, Bridget didn't know anything about flowers or groundhogs or past sadnesses and happenings. Doc was the one who could help me figure things out.

I showed him the bracelet the next day. I told him how everyone had gotten so stiff and uncomfortable after the restaurant. But I couldn't tell the how-come of what happened because I wouldn't really understand it myself until the night of Mama's party.

So I expect that's why Doc gave me a bad bit of advice. He was seeing things for half of what they were, like a jigsaw puzzle with a lot of pieces missing.

"Nice bracelet," Doc had grunted. "Look, Alice, make sure you behave yourself at that party. Try your hardest to be a little lady. Talk to Mr. Barker like you have something to say. Don't be asking too many questions. I know you're always looking for a way to make your mama happy. This is it. She's finally showing some sense. Mr. Barker has two feet on the ground—not like that fly-by-night father of yours. You hear?"

"Yes, sir. Sometimes I forget how to act right, though, Doc. And sometimes even when I'm doing what I think is right—like being nice to that mother and daughter yesterday—I get in trouble."

"What mother and daughter are you talking about, child?" I knew he hadn't heard a word I'd said. I started to fill him in, but his impatience was running things now. Doc held up his hand. "Never mind. Stick to the subject. Just remember to watch and learn; listen before you talk. People are a lot like roses. They'll show you what they need to open up."

Felt like everyone was telling me not to mess up. I wasn't looking forward to this party at all. "I wish you were going to be there, Doc."

"A fancy party is no place for me, child. Edna will be in the kitchen if you need her."

"Doc, if I say something stupid tomorrow night, you'll still like me, right? You won't get mad at me like you did with Mama, will you?"

He put his rough, weather-beaten old hand on my shoulder and smiled at me gently. "Alice, I'm not going to be around forever. You need to get to a good place with your mother. You do that for me, so I'll stop worrying about you so much." He patted me. "Now, go on, scoot. I've got more roses to bring in."

I was watching Mama put on her makeup for the party, enjoying a fresh breeze that danced through the bathroom window, tossing the organza curtains. The night before, a wild thunderstorm had scrubbed the earth clean. The mustard haze of humidity was gone, and a crystal blue sky capped the world. It was an absolutely beautiful evening.

"I can't believe how lucky we are, can you, Alice?" Mama chirped as she leaned over the sink to inspect her pencil-thin eyebrows.

"No, Mama, I can't."

The house had been completely ready since noon. You'd have thought the president was coming with all the hurrah going on. Lining the patio were tables that Edna had covered with table linens she had starch-ironed to a crisp. She'd washed our Limoges china until it was squeaky white and polished the silverware until it glinted. The hardwood floors gleamed from paste wax Doc had rubbed into them. He'd washed the tall windows, too, so the baubles in the old handblown glass showed tiny rainbows as the sun streamed through.

But what made the house drop-dead gorgeous were Doc's roses. They were everywhere—in huge cut-glass vases, in gleaming Jefferson silver bowls; in tall, narrow bud vases; on top of the piano, the tables, the mantles, the bookshelves. The house was a bower. And the garden was still just jumping with blooms.

Frank Sinatra crooned "Come Fly with Me" on the record player. I was already in my party dress, its Peter Pan collar cutting into my neck. I had decided that the light blue fabric screamed baby dress, even if Caroline Kennedy had worn the very same outfit. My feet were smashed into patent-leather Mary Janes—the kind of shoes I'd worn when I was three years old.

Mama had pulled the front part of my hair up in a bow and curled the rest exactly the way she'd promised. But it just kinked out in ringlets and spikes. "Oh, dear," she had said, yanking on it. "Well, the humidity will pull it out soon enough into a nice wave." Of course, this was the first day since June that the air was totally clear. Those stupid cabbage-like curls were there to stay all night.

Mama wore a simple, sleeveless shift, set off with a double strand of pearls. That's what all the mothers wore to parties. But she looked different in it than most of her friends did. Mama was petite and fit and definitely had curves. The hot pink material of her dress clung as she turned. What I really wanted were her sandals. Her toes slipped through a string of hot pink beads, free and comfortable. Plus, the shoes made a pretty *click-click* as she walked, announcing her coming like a nice perfume does.

"You look beautiful, Mama," I said.

She smiled, still concentrating on her reflection in the mirror.

I propped my elbows on the sink's white porcelain and completely forgot my rule about not disturbing her with questions about my father. "Did Daddy think you were pretty?"

"Well . . . he always said so. And I think he meant it."

"Betcha he'd say so tonight."

Mama tilted her head to look at the sheen of her hair. It was poufed up slightly and flipped out at the ends. "I'm not sure he would like my hairdo. He always liked it long and wavy. That was the hardest thing for me to get it to do. I had to perm it. Lord, did it stink. But

that's the way he liked it. So that's the way I wore it."
She straightened her dress and smiled. "I happen to
know that Mr. Barker likes pink the color of sloe-gin
fizzes."

She turned away from the mirror to look at me.
"You're wearing that bracelet Mr. Barker gave you,
aren't you?"

I held up my arm to show it dangling there.

"Good girl."

She patted my hand, and I grabbed hers before it
slipped away. Her rings were all askew on her slender
fingers. I straightened them. The diamond on the ring
my father had given her was a tiny dot, and I tried to
rub it into being shinier and bigger. I know she still
wore it because Virginia society said that's what a
widow should do, no matter how young she was.

"How did Daddy propose to you?"

"Oh, Alice, I don't have time to tell you that right
now."

"Pleeeeeease," I held tight to her hand.

She sighed and gave in, seeing it would take less time
to tell than argue. "It was up in the mountains, on the
Skyline Drive. Cold as could be. He'd driven me up
there in his convertible. Lyle loved the wind. He could
talk such nonsense, but this time, he was different,
almost like he was afraid. He told me that he'd seen a lot
of trouble, a lot of horror in Korea. And that he'd done
a lot of things that haunted him." Mama sat down on

the window ledge, and her voice cracked a little. "He spoke poetry. He said that he was having trouble touching down, that he couldn't find a safe runway anywhere, except with me. He said if I'd have him, he'd be able to fly straight. And that we'd live in the clouds, just he and I."

Two tears crept out of Mama's blue eyes and dropped onto her skirt: *Plip-plop.* The sound seemed to break a trance. She glanced down slowly but jumped up as fast as if I had jabbed her with a pin. "Oh no."

The tears had soaked themselves in her mascara, dragging black inkish smudges down her face and staining her dress. She grabbed a washcloth and dabbed at the fabric. All that did was leave two nasty gray blotches across her tummy.

"Oh, for pity's sake." Mama shoved me toward the door. "Always asking me questions. I don't want to be thinking about your father tonight, Alice. Can't you let me be happy? It's time I take off these rings anyway." She yanked them off and tossed them onto the windowsill, where they rolled and spun like little tops.

Afraid they might fall and slip behind the radiator, I lunged to catch them and instead knocked over her cologne bottle. Sweet cinnamon-colored liquid *glugged* out over her makeup, turning her face powder to mud. "Alice!" Mama scrambled to right the bottle but the damage was done. She slammed her hand onto the sink. "Go on, get out of here and leave me in peace."

"But, Mama, I didn't mean to . . ."

"Get out! You've always brought me trouble!"

She pushed me through and banged the bathroom door shut, leaving me locked out, facing a full-length mirror. "You are such a loser," I hissed at the frightened, stupid girl standing there.

"Honey bunch, where you hiding?" Edna's voice called through the darkness of my room.

I didn't answer. I'd figured if I stayed locked up in my room, I couldn't do any more harm. I was standing behind the flowery curtains, trying to keep from sneezing at the dust in them. My room hadn't gotten the same work-over the rest of the house had for the party. I was pressed against the open window, listening to the sound of people arriving—crunching gravel, quick nervous hello laughs, and the front screen door opening and closing. Below my feet, in the big parlor, a pianist tuned up with a bass and a guitar player, then began playing "Moon River."

"Alice, your mama wants you downstairs right now." Edna clicked on the light.

I still didn't answer.

"Now where could that child be?" Edna mused. "Hmmmmmmmm."

I recognized the voice she'd used when I was really little and we'd played hide-and-seek in the kitchen while she made meals. But this time I *really* didn't want her to find me.

She moved closer to the window. "Oh, my, oh, my. Here are Alice's shoes. Do you suppose she's gone off barefoot? I better get those shoes and . . ." Edna pulled back the curtain and pretended to be surprised, "Why, lookee what I found."

"I'm not a baby, Edna. I don't fall for that stuff anymore: 'Golly gee whiz, look what's here.' " I made a rude face.

"Well, then, don't act like a baby," Edna was gentle but firm. "Since you're so growed up, you can come down and be a good hostess—no matter what happened up here with your mama."

"I can't."

"Yes, you can. Here's what you do," she pulled me away from the window. "Take a deep breath. Stand up tall and straight. Don't ever stand like a whipped puppy." She lengthened herself up several inches as she drew in a big, long breath, and I did the same, following her. "Don't be worrying about what people say about you or to you. Remember you're a child of God and as such, equal to a queen. That's what I always told my children. Carry yourself with pride, and the hurts people throw at you will bounce right off. And you know what?"

"What?" I asked, the pout still in my voice.

"They'll treat you better when they see your dignity. And if you answer fire with cool, the fire goes out because there's nothing to feed it. Reverend King taught us that. And we've got to remember it, now that he's gone, now that there's so much trouble. We shall overcome if we just keep our heads. You, too, Alice."

Reluctantly, I puffed up my chest. I didn't believe her really, but at least I could please Edna.

"That's my honey lamb. Now, come on. I've got a kitchen to run." She took my hand and led me to the top of the landing. A knot of people was at the bottom of the stairs around Mama. Edna took two steps back. "G'on, Miss Alice," she whispered.

Slowly, I stepped down two stairs, my humiliating Mary Jane shoes tapping loudly on the hardwood. All the adults turned 'round.

"There you are." My mother's voice sounded merry, but her eyes still said mad. She was wearing a different dress, same cut, but mint green—not Mr. Barker's favorite color.

"Aaaaaaaw, isn't she just darling," one of the ladies *oohed*. "That outfit makes her look just like a little doll. Come here, honey, and turn around so I can get a good look at you. My daughter refuses to dress in anything pretty anymore. Oh, Grace, she's delicious." The old crow actually pinched my cheek.

It was going to be a long, long night.

CHAPTER SIXTEEN

find something
worth talking about

There was no hiding in the kitchen. Edna had
recruited several cousins, a son, and a son-in-law to
serve the guests. The place was like a gigantic anthill—
bodies carrying food and bumping into each other as
they scurried back and forth. The food coming out of
the kitchen was tremendous—old Virginia ham bis-
cuits, fresh-shucked oysters, little chicken salad and
watercress sandwiches, and bite-sized crab cakes. There
was about enough for the whole county.

I waded through rumpled suits and wildly bright
sundresses. Mixed all together, the smells were sicken-
ing—cigarettes; spicy aftershave; talcum powder; heavy
perfumes of magnolia, lily of the valley, and gardenia;

plus the icky-sticky sweetness of bourbon. I saw everything about chest height of the adults—the stains on their ties, the gold bracelets on their wrists, the bulge at their belts, the tilt of Waterford tumblers. Every once in a while, I saw mint green flash by, heard the musical tinkle of Mama's laugh, and knew she was at least sailing the same ocean I was.

People were nice enough, I suppose. I nodded and smiled a lot when they told me I looked just like Mama, or just like my grandmother, or just like my grandfather, even some great-great aunt I'd never heard tell of before. No one mentioned my daddy.

I finally saw Mr. Barker on the patio. He was standing next to his wrinkled old grandmother who had taken a wrought-iron throne on the edge of the party, by the garden's beginnings. Guests came by twos and threes to pay her respect and then hustled off as soon as they could, while I timed my escape into the growing twilight of the yard.

"Alice." I felt Mama's hand, heavy, on my shoulder. "I want you to go chat with Mr. Barker now and meet his grandmother. Be your best self. She's definitely the matriarch of the county."

I had no idea what a matriarch was, but it sounded important. Okay, I thought, if I do the party thing right, Mama won't be mad at me anymore. I let her guide me by my shoulders, even though I could have walked without being led. "Here's Alice, Bill. Mrs. Barker, I'd like you to meet my daughter, Alice."

"Yes, indeed. What a pretty dress," Mrs. Barker croaked at me. She looked to be 180 years old. Her dark eyes were big and pretty, but her skin hung in layers around her neck, and her hands were doubled over on themselves, which must have hurt. I didn't try to shake her hand hello. "Are you enjoying yourself, Alice?"

"Yes, ma'am. Thank you, ma'am. Hey, Mr. Barker. I love my bracelet. See, I've got it on. It was really nice of you to give it to me." I looked to Mama and was rewarded with a smile.

Mr. Barker looked even taller and darker to me tonight, but maybe it was because he was standing half in shadow, half in light. He was especially dandied up for the party. His black hair was parted and combed back severely, and he kept fiddling with a pocket watch that stretched between his vest pockets. He held one of those funny triangular glasses with a long stem. Back in the kitchen, Edna's son had called the drink a martini as he poured a whole lot of liquor into it and topped it off with an olive. Mr. Barker's was already empty.

My eyes traveled back to his face. He smiled down at me. "Glad to see you, Alice. You look pretty tonight. With a little work, you might even look a little like your mama here. Although it'll be tough to compete with Grace." He claimed her with an arm across her shoulder.

"Oh, now, Bill, you flatter me too much. I might get

a big head," Mama answered in that cocktail-hour way of joking. "Besides, Alice has her own good looks." Mama nervously petted my kinked-out hair. She never did that. My pulse banged in my ears.

"We were just admiring your rose garden," Mrs. Barker said to Mama, "and this lovely arrangement here." A bowl of blossoms sat on the table beside her. "I don't recognize this bud, dear. Its scent is so wonderful, almost like fruit. What is it?"

Mama hesitated. I knew she had no idea.

"Oh, oh, oh, I know, Mrs. Barker," I blurted. This was my chance to make up for the disaster in Mama's bathroom. "It's Tropicana. It's a pretty new rose. I bet you haven't got one. Doc just put it into the garden a few years ago, and it's beautiful, isn't it? But it gets nasty black-spot all over and spreads it to every other rose. Just like Typhoid Mary spreading disease. I studied about her in school. See these scars?" I held my arms up and kept on talking lickety-split. "I got them picking up black-spot leaves. You have to do that, you know, spraying isn't enough."

Doc would be so proud of me. I'd found something worth talking about, just like he'd told me to. I pushed the bowl toward Mrs. Barker. "See this one, that's a Mr. Lincoln. There's a Dainty Bess. That one, too. My Grandmother planted that rose with Doc. Did you know her?" I forgot to wait for an answer. "This one's Iceberg. I don't much like the name, but Doc says it's good because its white color is so pure and strong. I love this dark pink one. It's called Nearly Wild. Doc says that rose must have been named after me."

I heard Mama clear her throat. Mr. Barker shifted his feet around loudly. I stopped short, realizing I was talking way, way too much.

Only Mrs. Barker smiled reassuringly. "My goodness, child, you're a regular rosarian. Grace, you must join the Garden Club so that Alice can become a junior member. We'd all learn a lot from her."

Mama looked relieved—until Mr. Barker spoke up: "You'd never get anything done at the meetings, Granna. Alice can talk a blue streak you wouldn't believe. She'll talk to anyone who will listen. In fact, she about gave an engraved invitation to a colored woman to take the front-window table at Jake's restaurant the other day. Jake gave me heck about alienating his best customers."

"Oh, Bill, surely that didn't cause him trouble," Mama said. "All that upset over lunch counters is long done with, isn't it? I remember the boycott of that all-white movie theater on the Corner and that Memorial Day sit-in at the restaurant on Emmett Street. It was right before President Johnson signed the Civil Rights Act, and that was in 1964, I know. Four years ago. Jake should get used to it. Especially if he wants to do business with the students. They were the ones who organized the boycott and that sit-in and I hear there are some who are pushing for admitting more blacks to the college. There's a handful attending already, doing very well, I hear. Children Alice's age go to school together. Seems a lot better if you ask me. I remember passing the colored school when I was little and it was a disgrace."

Mr. Barker rolled his eyes, put down his glass, and stuck his hands in his pockets—a sure sign of a lecture coming. And boy, was it a doozie.

"Grace, you're not a closet liberal, are you? You clearly don't understand how tense things are these days. Yes, it's law. That woman can eat wherever she wants to. But that doesn't mean people like Jake *like* it. He was a big supporter of Governor Almond's 'massive resistance' that shut down public schools in Charlottesville rather than integrate them. Remember that? Jake and his friends sure do. Especially now that there's been all this rioting and rise in militant groups' rhetoric. American cities went up in flames when King was shot—one hundred and sixty-eight of them, Grace. Detroit, Chicago, Kansas City, Oakland, Baltimore. Part of Washington, D.C., is still smoldering. They set seven hundred separate fires around 14th Street. That's just a few blocks from the White House."

"Such a shame," his grandmother murmured, shaking her head. "There were some beautiful buildings there. And there were lots of colored storeowners who lost everything because their own people looted them. It made no sense to me. Right before Easter, too. *Tsk, tsk.*" She looked off into the darkness, and said more to herself than the others, "I went to hear King speak when he came to Cabell Hall. Right before that marvelous march on Washington in 1963. You know, when he stood on the steps of the Lincoln Memorial and said he had a dream that one day we would judge one another by the content of our character, not the color of our skin. Only one of my bridge-club ladies would come with me to hear King. I remember him saying that privileged groups seldom give up their privileges voluntarily. That's worried me ever since. You know, dear," she looked up at Grace, "only one administrator of the university attended that speech. I'm not sure that the university officially backed it."

For a moment, Mr. Barker looked down at his grand-mother in stunned silence. But then he just continued his tirade. "The important thing is King's nonviolent philosophy isn't running things anymore, Grace. Most say his control over his people died a couple of years ago anyway. That march on Washington you're so taken with, Granna, well, his political rival, Malcolm X, had complete contempt for it. He called it 'the farce on Washington.' Radicals like Stokely Carmichael and those Black Panthers run things now. They say their people are 'human combustion.' Their 'black power' means black revolution. Malcolm X's motto was 'by any means necessary.' They mean it. Don't you doubt it."

"Things are settling down, though, aren't they, Bill?" Mama tried.

He gave her a *duuuuuh* look. "No, they're not, Grace.

125

It's only spreading to people who should know better. Haven't you seen the television coverage of the riots going on in Chicago this weekend? The city's full of LSD-popping college kids throwing bags of urine and rocks at the police who are trying to protect the Democrats as they choose a candidate for president. Do you know how few countries have the right to choose candidates to begin with? Counterculture, my eye. This country is completely out of control.

"I'm okay with civil rights, Grace, but I'm not going to act like a big proponent of it either. I'm running for state office next fall. The Byrd family has held Virginia's senate seat since the 1930s, not because they created Virginia conservatism, but because they saw it and reflected it. I need to do the same, no matter what might be happening on UVA grounds or in a few gentlewomen's bridge clubs. A lot of voters still hold with Alabama Governor George Wallace—'segregation now, tomorrow, and forever.' People are scared. And when they're scared they give up on whatever progressive ideals they were toying with. Wallace's hard-nosed, third-party candidacy for president is gaining a lot of momentum given the riots. They say he may carry as many as five southern states."

"But, Bill . . ."

"But nothing, Grace. You stick to what you know—throwing beautiful garden parties and gussying yourself up for them—and we'll be just fine."

I felt sick. Mama looked like kids do at school when a teacher corrects them, taking pains to make sure the rest of the class knew just how stupid their answer had been.

I glanced at Mrs. Barker. She looked like she felt sorry for Mama. But she didn't say anything.

This was my fault. I'd set up Mama to be eaten alive, like opening the door of a chicken coop to a fox. I tried to steer things back to the roses. I'd been doing fine with them. "Do you grow roses, Mr. Barker?"

Everyone looked startled that I'd spoken. I think they'd forgotten I was standing there.

"I'm too busy to mess around with flowers, Alice. I've got real business to tend to."

I frowned. "Well, what would you like to talk about, Mr. Barker?" Nervousness made me say about the dumbest thing I could: "I'm supposed to talk about something interesting, so you'll like me and marry Mama."

"Alice," gasped Mama.

I slapped a hand over my mouth. Mrs. Barker covered hers, too, and I swear I heard her giggle.

Edna saved me. She arrived, carrying drinks on one of her sparkling silver trays—an old-fashioned for Mrs. Barker, Dubonnet for Mama, and another big martini for Mr. Barker.

Immediately, Mr. Barker grabbed his glass and took a loud gulp. "*UUUGH*," he made a face. "Edna, take this martini back to the bar, and tell them to make a real one. I suffered through the first, but now I want a good martini. Tell them to make it dry—with gin and just a dash of vermouth. This one's swimming in it."

As she stepped to the door to return the drink, Mr. Barker boomed in his forever-big voice, "The colored never know how to make a good martini. But I suppose I shouldn't expect them to know about good liquor. Rotgut wine is probably more their speed."

My mouth dropped open. I don't think he meant Edna to hear it. I think he was making a stupid joke. But she heard all right.

Edna froze in the doorway, her back to us. I watched it straighten, Edna's calm making her seem enormously tall. She turned slightly and said quietly, "No, Mr. Barker, sir, we just know better than to down that much strong liquor in one drink." Then she glided away.

"What?" Mr. Barker's face looked like a bulldog's. "Did you hear that, Grace? Do you condone that kind of behavior? We're going to have to have a serious discussion about how you manage Alice in public and what type of help you employ."

I turned to Mama, silently begging her to tell him off. He didn't just think he was better than the hired help, like Bridget did, he thought he was better than Mama.

But Mama didn't. She just forced a smile and excused herself with a slight bow of her head. "I need to check on my other guests, Bill. Please excuse me, Mrs. Barker. I'll be back."

I thought I would throw up. Mama was doing the same thing I did when Bridget had hurt Edna's feelings—*nothing*. I was used to her not defending me. But this was Edna. And Mama wasn't even standing up for herself. Well, I guess I had to. "Edna doesn't drink, Mr. Barker," I said, clenching my fists. "Not like some people I see around here. And Mama knows about a lot of things besides throwing parties."

I ran through the door before he could answer, hot after Mama, clipping her heels. I was afraid, afraid that she might actually fire Edna because her new important beau didn't like her. "Mama," I whispered loudly. "Mama. Aren't you going to say something to him?"

"No."

"But Mama."

She stopped short and I crashed into her. "Alice, we are not going to discuss this now. We know how wonderful Edna is. Lord, she's practically raised you, and me, for that matter. I'd never fire her. But I'm not going to make a big fuss about it, either, especially during a party with the whole town watching."

She walked away. Her mint green shift disappeared into a wave of fancy dresses and suits as her party swallowed her up.

Doc was right. Mama was failing her tests. Big time.

CHAPTER SEVENTEEN

birds hate to be caged

I found my way to the corner of the rose garden and ripped his stupid bracelet off. I kicked and kicked and kicked until it was covered with dirt.

From there I could see his grandmother, sitting stonelike, and Mr. Barker going back and forth between the party and her. I knelt to watch. Once they talked for a long time. Mr. Barker drank another of those drinks then. That was three martinis that I knew of. I couldn't believe he was still standing.

Daddy may have been unpredictable and dangerous and mad when Mama argued with him. But I didn't see how Mr. Barker was going to be so much safer. He was in control, but it just seemed like controlled meanness to me. And if he didn't like Edna and her opinions, he sure wasn't going to like Doc's. He obviously didn't care a lick for Mama's or mine.

Just as I figured all that out and was starting to feel real clammy, inside and out, I heard his campaign-stump voice rip through the party chatter.

"Gather 'round, please," he thundered. He waved the musicians to stop playing and the cocktail party eased down into silence. I didn't like the look of things and tiptoed to the open French doors of the living room.

"I want witnesses," he continued. "Grace? Grace, where are you? Come on up here."

Mama had been in the kitchen and people had to call back to her. She emerged, flustered, and slipped through the crowd. Mr. Barker reached out and pulled her into him kind of roughly because she tripped a little before fitting up under his arm. "First, we should all thank this pretty lady for a lovely evening. Don't you think, folks?"

Applause answered him. He beamed. I swear he looked like a bullfrog that'd just snapped up a big, juicy fly. Mama nodded and smiled—not saying a word even though it was her party—just like I'd seen Mrs. Nixon do while her sweaty-faced husband campaigned for president.

"Now, I have some important business here," Mr. Barker boomed on. "You all know I've long been look-ing for the right little woman for me—a gal who can help me achieve the dreams I have for the common-wealth, who will support my work, plus," he winked and said, "be a good eye-catcher for the press."

Someone cat-whistled.

"I was lucky enough to fall in love with Grace here. She fills all my hopes and dreams. Her name is very appropriate, don't you think?"

"Yes, indeed," shouted one man. There was more happy hand clapping.

I felt myself inching through the crowd to see my mother's face.

"Well, then," Mr. Barker went on, playing the crowd. He was good at playing them. I could see him stirring a mob up into just about anything. He'd gotten me with a charm bracelet and a smile, hadn't he? "I'm going to ask her to marry me right now. Do you think I should?"

"Yes, yes!" called some guests.

"You've got to help me now!" he shouted.

"We will!"

He reached in his pocket and turned to Mama, although his face still tipped toward the party mob. "This was the ring my father gave my mother when they became engaged, and I thought it fitting I should give it to my bride. Will you wear it, Grace, and be mine?"

Mama's face was aflame, the color of her ruined pink dress. I held my breath. What could she be thinking? The whole thing felt like an auction at the county fair. Don't do it, Mama, I pleaded silently. I tried to get her to look at me. *Don't do it.*

Some man started chanted, "Yes, yes, yes . . ." and others picked it up.

I cried out over it, "Mama?"

Only a couple of guests heard me and made way. I stepped forward and called again, louder, "Mama!"

Mr. Barker glared at me and made a gesture so that the man standing next to me put a firm hand on my shoulder. "Not now, Alice," the man warned.

Mama didn't give me one glance. She nodded and the party broke into cheers and applause.

"Isn't this exciting?" one woman tittered.

"Her mother would be thrilled," her friend answered.

Mr. Barker held up the engagement ring for everyone to see, took Mama's hand, and slipped the jewel on her finger. The same finger she'd had Daddy's ring on just a few hours ago.

I didn't really know my daddy. Given what Doc and Mama had told me, I wasn't sure I'd have been happy if I had. But I knew for sure that I didn't want this man as my stepdaddy. Seemed like Mama was just swapping one bossy man for another. Mr. Barker was way too impressed with himself and what he thought. He'd try to keep people like Edna down just because that's what he figured voters wanted, and he didn't have the gump-tion to lead them to change. He'd keep my mama down. He'd tell her how to talk, how to dress, how to think— even about me. She'd completely disappear into him.

I couldn't stand the thought of it.

Out of my gut a cry boiled up: "Don't do it, Mama! Please, don't!"

The party went dead silent, icing me over. It was like one of those bad nightmares when everything quick-freezes into a horrible, still picture. A hundred pair of eyes stared at me. There was no waking up from this one.

Finally, Mr. Barker spoke. "Well," he said with a not-real laugh. "Anybody know of a good boarding school?"

The guests laughed and the still picture broke. People pushed forward to congratulate Mama and Mr. Barker. No one spoke to me. Heck, no one came within ten feet of me. I stood rooted, dying. I'd lost Mama for sure.

"Honey bunch," I heard Edna's voice, and I turned to look up at her. There she was again with that silver tray and her quiet calm. "Come back into the kitchen, honey. There's some cake back there you'll like."

Her voice started a trickle of life through my frozen body. I tried to smile at her, but my mouth just quivered and my vision of her blurred with tears.

"No need for that, Edna." Mr. Barker came out of nowhere to stand over me. "Alice and I are going to have a nice little chat." That thick, hard hand curled itself around my arm, and I felt myself pulled out the door, over the patio, down the walk to the back rose garden.

I stumbled along the ground and tripped on the flag-stones. The hand never let go, the walk never slowed, and Mr. Barker never spoke until he whirled me around to face him. He leaned over so that his nose and those big, dark, angry eyes were only inches from mine. His breath came hot and ugly, stinking of booze.

"You better learn your place, girlie," he growled. "Children in my family respect their elders. They don't talk out of turn. You don't have anything to say about my marrying your mother."

He straightened, like he was done.

Somewhere inside my head, Doc grunted. *Stand up for what you believe, child.*

I glared up at Mr. Barker and managed to squeak out, "Do, too. She's my mama."

He came down into my face again. "You better forget about existing. You're just like that no-good father of yours, making demands you've no right to. I met him. He was a worthless, big-talking flyboy with no education, no background, no future, just a way with women. What do you think it's been like for your mother having to look at you all the time—a reminder of how he degraded her? I bet she feels sick when she looks at you. I would."

I was trembling so hard my teeth chattered. I knew he was drunk, and drunks could be vicious, going after you like a junkyard dog grabs a rabbit by the jugular and shakes it 'til its neck snaps. Mr. Barker had a good hold on my soul by my fear that Mama really didn't want me, couldn't possibly love me. I slapped my hands over my ears, but I heard him.

In the corner of my eye, I noticed a shadowy figure, backlit by the patio's party lights. But I paid it no mind. All I could focus on was the voice that was ripping me apart.

"Think I was joking about boarding school?" Mr. Barker ranted on. "I'm gonna find one that knows about disciplining a smart-mouthed kid. One that will whip you into shape. But you aren't ever going to amount to much, no matter what we do, girlie, because you're the baby of a deadbeat."

"That's enough." The voice was afraid and small. My ears were ringing, so I couldn't recognize it.

Mr. Barker held his hand up to shade his eyes against the lights. When he recognized the figure, it didn't even faze him. "That's not enough, Grace," he said, dismissing Mama. "I can tell you haven't disciplined this child at all. It's obviously not in your nature. But I know how to handle a kid like this. I bet what she's needed all along is a good, hard spanking." He pulled back his hand as if he might wallop me right then and there.

"Get away from her, Bill!"

He hesitated. "I won't be humiliated by your first husband's daughter in front of my people, Grace. I won't be talked to like this. You have to make a choice."

"A choice?" Mama repeated the word with a kind of hushed horror. "A choice?" Then she said, "I've heard that before, Bill. Alice, honey, you come here to me."

I wrenched myself free and flew to her, wrapping my arms around her waist. She was shaking, too. But she kept on talking. "I think you're right, Bill. I need to make a choice." She pulled his ring off her finger and held it toward him. "I've been bullied enough in my life. My choice is to not make another mistake. Alice is not quite eleven and has more insight and courage than I do. It's time I follow her lead and stand up for myself and for her."

"What?" he sneered. "You can't be serious." He refused to take the ring. "I'll just wait until you come to your senses." He crossed his arms across his chest.

She reached out for his hand. "Don't touch him, Mama," I cried, holding tight.

"Don't worry, Alice. I have come to my senses all right, Bill." She tucked the ring into Mr. Barker's breast pocket. "Good-bye, Bill. It won't take you long to find another stage prop. The room in there is full of them."

He gaped at her and then hissed, "People were right about you, Grace. You're a fool. No one does me this way. You haven't heard the last of it."

He pushed past us and crashed through the rosebushes.

We stood there, holding each other. After a while, Mama said, "Alice, don't you believe what he said about you."

"I won't, Mama, if you say not to. I love you, Mama."

"I love you, too, Alice. I always have. I think I just forgot how to show it." She paused. "Thank you, Alice."

"What for, Mama?"

"For showing me something important. That would have been a pretty cage to be in, but it would have been a cage all the same. I always hate to see a bird in a cage, don't you, honey?"

"Yes, ma'am. They're happier being able to fly wherever they want, aren't they?"

"Yes, they are." I felt her pull herself up just like Edna had told me to do before. "It's time for me to stop singing just for easy feed and a pretty perch."

Mama stepped back and took my hands in hers. "Tell you what. That party will run itself. Why don't we sneak into the kitchen, grab a piece of cake, and come back out here and look at the stars, just you and me."

Edna cut us both huge hunks. It was the best piece of cake I've ever tasted.

CHAPTER EIGHTEEN

tuck memories away
for eternity

"Tell me again what happened?" Doc asked the next morning.

I told him.

"*Whew,*" he took off his hat and scratched his head. "Don't that beat all. Good for Miss Grace. I had no idea Bill Barker could be such a jackass." Then he put his arm around me and said quietly, "I'm proud of you, Alice. Proud of you for standing up for Edna and your mama."

We were sitting in the wheelbarrow together. He and I were the only ones around. Edna had the day off. Mama was still asleep. Doc had come at daybreak to check his roses to make sure "no ding-blasted fool had trampled them." I'd seen him from my window and come down to join him. My bare feet were cool as they brushed back and forth across the dew-covered grass, but it was clear that the heat was going to come back again harsh.

"You know what, Doc?"

"What?"

"I did like talking to that old Mrs. Barker."

"Yes?"

"She seemed real interested in your roses. I told her all about the roses and you."

"You did?"

"Yep. I was telling her all the names and what you thought about them. She seemed real impressed."

"That a fact?"

"Yes, sir. Make you feel good, Doc?"

But he didn't answer me. "There he is again," he muttered, reaching down for a rake. "Can you believe that GD groundhog, checking out the patio for leftovers?"

Doc *eeeeeeked* his way out of the wheelbarrow, his joints creaking almost as loudly as the wheelbarrow's. "Hey," he waved the rake and bellowed his usual battle cry. "Hey, you!" Doc took a step forward, getting ready to jog after his enemy.

But he stopped and snorted. "Can't keep that rodent down, nohow. Ever seen an animal that fat and sassy?" It was grudging, but it was respect in Doc's voice for sure. Maybe even a weird kind of affection. Big Tom sat up.

They gazed at one another like two old stubborn knights who enjoyed whacking the heck out of each other.

Doc sighed. "Better move him on, though." He took a step and then turned to wink at me. He held his rake up like a lance and shouted, "Charge!"

I giggled as he started to trot, pretending to be on a horse.

Doc only got a few feet. He cried out and clutched his chest.

"Doc, what's the matter?" I cried.

Doc gasped and coughed. Roughly, he grabbed my shoulder to steady himself, but we both toppled to the ground.

I squirmed out from under him and looked down at him. His old tanned face was white as that Iceberg rose. "Doc, Doc, what's the matter?"

He grimaced like someone was pulling a carving knife through his innards. I stood up and screamed, "Mama! Mama!"

Her window opened, and Mama's sleep-dazed face peered out.

"Something's wrong with Doc!"

I dropped to my knees and started fanning him with my hands, with his hat, with leaves. "Doc! Doc, talk to me!"

I heard Mama rush up behind me, her bare feet slapping the flagstone walk. "Oh, Lord." She reached down and undid the top buttons on his shirt. "Doc," she spoke to him loudly, "I'm going to call an ambulance. Hang on." And she was gone.

Doc's eyes opened and struggled to focus. I saw him scan the sky, the tops of the maple trees, the house, and then he turned to his roses. A small smile spread on his face. I could tell he was memorizing everything—every cloud, every leaf, every brick, every blossom—like he was tucking the vision away for eternity. Like he was saying good-bye.

"Doc," I whispered. "Don't you leave me."

Slowly, Doc dragged his eyes from his beloved garden back to me. He blinked hard three times to find my face. Then he held fast to it, even as we waited twenty minutes for the ambulance to come, even as the medics lifted him up into the back of the van. As they gently pushed me back from him to close the doors, Doc whispered, "Remember. Prune my roses. I've kept them growing for you. All I have to give you."

"Yes, Doc," I sobbed.

Doc lingered, slowly shrinking, in the hospital for several weeks. The nurses said he'd had a massive heart attack that brought on a stroke. He was paralyzed on one side, and there'd been what they called brain damage. I went to see him a couple of times each week. School had started, and Mama had to drive me all the way into Charlottesville to the university hospital. She'd sit outside his room, waiting for me.

At first, it scared me visiting Doc. He was so silent, like he wasn't completely there. But he recognized me half the time. I could tell by the way his eyes snapped in on me and stayed there that I was what kept him hanging on. Slowly, I realized that I was the one who had to let him go. His time of beauty was over.

So, the last week of September, I picked an armload of his roses. I made sure I had all his favorites—Mr. Lincoln, Peace, Dainty Bess, even Tropicana. As I walked down the hall, their lovely scent blocked out the stink of antiseptics and medicine. The staff had moved Doc beside a window, and he was staring out it, breathing hard and slow. His eyes were unblinking, and I couldn't tell what he looked at, if anything.

"Angels," said the nurse, patting me on the back. "I like to think they see angels when they don't seem to look at us anymore. Go on, sweetie. I think he's been waiting on you."

I put the huge bouquet beside him on the bed and pulled up my chair. "Hey, Doc, I've brought you some of your roses. They're in their best form right now. Mama helped me pick them." I took his old, splotchy hand in mine, and I felt just the tiniest squeeze back. He heard me even if he couldn't see me.

I took a deep breath. "You know, Doc, Mama and I are in a good place now, just like you wanted. I even got her to promise to help me take care of the roses. 'Cause I told her they were important to me. And she said she wanted to get to know about them because I loved them. And guess what? We played tennis together the other day—just Mama and me. Don't that beat all?"

Doc's breathing eased, but his eyes stayed fixed outside. I looked out at his view. Right then a huge flock of robins—maybe as many as a hundred—dropped down to the ground, just outside his window. "Birds are gathering now, Doc," I said more to myself than to him really. "Gathering to migrate for winter. I wonder how they always know when it's time to leave and how to get to where they're going." I turned back to look at him and saw him gazing right at me. I choked back tears and whispered our old joke, "Why do birds fly south, Doc? Remember? Because it's too far to walk."

The slightest smile eased across the side of his face that still worked. His eyes held mine and gleamed a kind of inside laugh. It was time to say good-bye while he still saw me for sure.

I inched my face right next to his. "It'll be just like flying south, Doc. You can't make the trip walking. You have to let go now and fly." I felt him shudder a tiny bit. I took another deep breath to steady myself. "Don't be afraid, Doc. God will be so glad to have such a fine gardener. I just know it."

Doc blinked, then closed his eyes, and left me.

The light from the window flickered with the shadows of all those birds suddenly taking off. I turned to watch and hoped they'd show him the way.

Afterword

I don't know that I'll ever have a good-bye as hard as that one. My throat still squeezes up when I think about it. But I know that Doc and I did right by each other. And when that door closed, another one opened, because Doc helped me find it. Mama and I are real close now.

I've tried to keep up the roses for Doc. I even talk to him while I weed the beds. Mama and I do a pretty decent job, although we've already got black-spot bad and it's only June. But the important thing is that we tend to the roses together. Mama's actually learned a few of the bushes' names. Our front hall table will always have at least a few blossoms on it June through

October. Seeing a pretty rose first thing in the morning just starts the day off right, I always say.

Things were pretty hot around town there for a while after Mama's party. Mr. Barker has a big mouth. But he's already found a nice, silent, blond fiancée. He's launched his campaign and everyone says he's a shoo-in, although there is a reporter from a local paper asking questions about Mr. Barker's drinking. Mama wonders if someone overheard him lighting into me at the party.

Bridget still writes once a week. I suspect she needs someone to sermonize to. I think she's kind of lonely, even at home. She says she's coming to Charlottesville again in July, but Mama and I both doubt that Mr. Barker's sister will let her spend any time with a trou-blemaker like me.

The real news is Mama is going to go back to college. And hopefully to the University of Virginia. Princeton and Yale have announced they're going to let in girl undergraduates for the very first time this fall. And Virginia doesn't like falling behind the Ivy Leagues, so there's talk they're going to admit girls to the College of Arts and Sciences in 1970. All the Virginia boys are in an uproar about it, saying it's going to wreck the honor system and distract them from studying. The worst are the alumni. They claim girls will pull down the academics and ruin UVA's reputation. A whole bunch of them are threatening to withdraw their yearly donations if the school lets girls in.

But change is going to come whether they like it or not. The whole world is getting evened up. Even for girls.

Right now Mama's working in the county library, shelving books. The pay is lousy, but she says she wants to get into the swing of school again and being around books is the best way. She wants to get an art or an English lit degree. She says she'll figure out how to make money later on.

Somebody's been talking to her about buying the back thirty acres to grow grapes for wine. I can't see that kind of crop growing well, but Mama says you never know. The cash certainly would set us up for a while. No matter what she decides, she's glad to have what she calls a man's decision to make on her own. Some day soon, I'm going to have to talk to Mama about this women's lib stuff I read about in *Seventeen*, a magazine Bridget sent me for Christmas.

Mama dates a little, but not much. Social invites definitely slacked off after she broke up with Mr. Barker. She says she doesn't care, though. She still sees one country-club type who compliments her looks plus a college professor who compliments her brains. She's just got to find a man who knows how to do both. Mostly, though, she stays home with me.

Edna doesn't come to the house anymore. After Doc died, she seemed to get real old, real fast. But I visit her.

She's happy because her grandchildren are with her most of the time. She always has a really wonderful dessert waiting when she knows I'm coming. Mama's taken to sitting and chatting. Listening to them talk, I realize that Edna and she always ate lunch together, too, when Mama was young. I guess when Mama became head of the house she thought she had to be something different.

The one thing that hasn't changed around our house is our having a groundhog. Strange how he stayed on after Doc died since Mama and I gave up growing vegetables. He just lives off grass these days, which makes me wonder why he had to bedevil poor Doc so much over his corn and tomatoes. I guess Doc's garden was just too tempting, like dangling a candy bar in front of a child.

Of course, I don't know for sure that it's Big Tom, the GD groundhog himself, or just one of his children. But this groundhog sure is big and bodacious. And, you know, he does the funniest thing at twilight. He waddles out to the rose garden and lies down there, almost like he's looking for Doc.

Maybe he is. I guess groundhogs don't know about flying south.

Laura Malone Elliott is the author of the acclaimed novel UNDER A WAR-TORN SKY. She is also the author of the picture book HUNTER'S BEST FRIEND AT SCHOOL, illustrated by Lynn Munsinger. She lives with her husband and their two children in Virginia.